Polly and the Prince

Polly and the Prince

Carola Dunn

THORNDIKE
CHIVERS

This Large Print edition is published by Thorndike Press®,
Waterville, Maine USA and by BBC Audiobooks Ltd,
Bath, England.

Published in 2005 in the U.S. by arrangement with Carola
Dunn.

Published in 2005 in the U.K. by arrangement with the author.

U.S. Hardcover 0-7862-8020-4 (Candlelight)
U.K. Hardcover 1-4056-3509-6 (Chivers Large Print)

The text of this Large Print edition is unabridged.
Other aspects of the book may vary from the original edition.

Set in 16 pt. Plantin by Al Chase.

Printed in the United States on permanent paper.

British Library Cataloguing-in-Publication Data available

Library of Congress Cataloging-in-Publication Data

Dunn, Carola.
    Polly and the prince / by Carola Dunn.
        p. cm. — (Thorndike Press large print candlelight)
    ISBN 0-7862-8020-4 (lg. print : hc : alk. paper)
    1. Large type books.   I. Title.   II. Thorndike Press large
print Candlelight series.
PR6054.U537P65 2005
823'.914—dc22   2005016372

To my mother, Margaret Brauer,
who did so much research for me
and who was my most loyal fan

1

Resting her heavy basket on the balustrade at the top of the steps leading down to the street, Polly gazed back at the Pantiles. She had often painted the scene, the colonnaded row of small shops and coffee houses which led to the Chalybeate Spring at the far end, yet it was slightly different each time she looked at it. At this hour in the morning, the trunks of the leafless lime trees cast interesting diagonal shadows across the clay-tiled walkway that gave the esplanade its name.

It was still early. The stout dowagers and crabby, gout-ridden gentlemen who would later stroll, or roll in Bath chairs, along the fashionable promenade of the little spa town were doubtless yet abed.

Polly smiled at an abigail, out exercising her mistress's Skye terrier. The shaggy little dog stopped and sniffed the air as the appetizing aroma of the fresh loaf Polly had just bought reached it. The maid tugged on its leash. It trotted on with many a backward glance, its quivering nose raised to catch the last whiff of that heavenly smell.

On twigs and boughs and swelling leaf buds, dewdrops hung sparkling in the limpid sunshine of late March. Rainbow gleams of pure red and blue and green caught Polly's eye. How could she capture that diamondlike glitter on canvas? She frowned as she visualized the effect of adding tiny dots of colour — it would probably just look odd, but it was worth trying.

Lost in thought she hefted her basket and started down the steps, scarcely aware of the tall, shabby man who stood courteously at the bottom, waiting hat in hand for her to pass before he started up.

Like the branches, the steps were damp with dew. Halfway down, Polly's foot slipped and caught in the hem of her skirt. With a cry of dismay she let go of the basket and tumbled headlong.

Strong arms arrested her fall, steadied her, released her.

"I'm so sorry," she gasped, straightening her bonnet. "Thank you, sir." She looked up into a smiling face, rather long and thin, weather bronzed, topped by curling, light brown hair. His merry hazel eyes slanted in a fascinatingly exotic way, demanding to be painted.

"Am very glad to be of service, *madame*."

Like his eyes, the stranger's voice was exotically foreign, with richly rolling 'r's.

Not French, Polly thought, despite the *"madame."* During her two years at school she had picked up a little French — in between as many art lessons as she was allowed to take — but that was ten years ago and more. Not that his accent mattered. His looks were what interested her. "Will you sit for me?" she asked eagerly.

"Sit?"

"Pose." Before she could explain further, the abigail appeared at the top of the steps.

"Oh miss, are you all right? I heard you cry out."

"I tripped but this man saved me." Polly beamed up at her, grateful for her concern.

The woman eyed the stranger's ill-fitting, threadbare garments with suspicion. "D'you know him, miss? You want to be careful . . ."

With a yelp of glee, the terrier yanked the leash from her grasp, scampered down the steps, and pounced on Polly's loaf, lying in the gutter beside the overturned basket. Then it backed away with a surprised look, sneezing and shaking its head.

The foreigner obligingly bent down to grab the end of its leash. As he straightened, Polly saw his nostrils twitch. She became aware that the odour of fresh bread had been replaced by pungent fumes so familiar she had not noticed them.

"My turpentine!" Heedless of the damage to the sage green skirts of her kerseymere pelisse, she dropped to her knees on the cobbles.

The basket lay on its side, but only the loaf and one brown glass bottle had actually fallen out. Though the bottle was unbroken, its stopper had come out and its contents flowed in a thin stream to the gutter, where the bread was soaking it up. Polly quickly replaced the stopper, sat back on her heels, and laughed at the thought of the dog's horror when it bit into the bread.

The abigail had run down to retrieve her unhappy charge from the suspect stranger. "Well, I'm sure there's no knowing what some folks think is proper," she muttered with a disdainful sniff that set her coughing as she stalked away, towed by the terrier, who was only too anxious to depart.

Polly laughed again. The man grinned down at her, his slanting eyes crinkling at the corners. From below he looked even taller, and very thin. Not weak, though. She had firsthand experience of the strength of the muscles concealed by the shapeless, out-at-elbows, brown fustian jacket from which his bare wrists protruded.

He knelt beside her, righted the basket, and took the bottle from her. His hands were rough and calloused, with splitting nails, but scrupulously clean.

"Turpentine?" he said as he carefully stowed it among the other packages. "*Skipidar*. And 'pose' is *pozirovat*. Now I know what you meant by 'sit.' " With one hand under her elbow he helped her rise, then picked up the basket. "You are artist, I think."

"Yes. I should like to paint your portrait. Your face is interesting."

"Eyes are different, *nyet?* I have Tatar ancestor."

"Tatar?"

"In English you say Tartar. They are Mongol peoples who ruled Russia for many centuries."

"You are Russian?" At his affirmative nod, Polly dismissed the subject as unimportant. "Will you sit for me? Are you staying long in Tunbridge Wells?" The canvas knapsack he carried slung over his shoulder suggested that he was travelling.

"Was my intention to stay only long enough to earn meal," he said doubtfully.

"You are hungry? I can give you something to eat if you come home with me.

11

Please come. It is not far, just a little way along Cumberland Walk."

He shrugged his shoulders. "I come then. Is no hurry, after all. Instead of washing dishes or sweeping floor, I sit for food like dog."

"Good dog!" In truth, Polly found the laughter in his eyes as attractive as their shape. "Let us go. I can come back tomorrow to have the turpentine bottle refilled."

"Is not necessary to buy bread?"

"Bread? Oh yes, I forgot. What a nuisance." She reached for the basket.

"Is too heavy," said the stranger firmly. "I carry."

"*Clever* dog," she said, then paused to watch two pigeons which flew down and landed near the loaf. One started busily foraging for crumbs. The other scuttled around its unconcerned mate, bowing and cooing, its neck feathers fluffed up in an iridescent ruff of purple and green. Like shot silk, Polly noted, and equally difficult to paint.

The Russian was offering his arm. For all his vagabond appearance he had gentlemanly instincts, she thought, laying her hand on the coarse-woven sleeve as they turned towards the steps. His English was excellent, too. She knew little about Russia, but she had had a vague impression that the peasants there were even less educated than the average English labourer.

Papa would have known. He had sailed the world's oceans for thirty years, rising from midshipman to captain, before succumbing to yellow fever in the Spice Islands. On his infrequent visits home he had told tales of a hundred lands, likely including Russia, but to Polly they had always seemed like fairytales, not solid information about real places. They were all mixed up in her head.

The bakery was in the center of the arcade. Three doors beyond it a sign announced "Bookseller — J. W. Irving — Printseller," the shop where Polly bought supplies for her painting.

"Since we are here, I might as well go in for the turpentine after all," she said, taking a shilling from her reticule. "Will you buy the bread? I daresay you had best get two loaves." She gave him the coin and went on.

As she waited for Mr. Irving to fill her bottle, it crossed her mind that the Russian now had the wherewithal to buy himself a good meal without the need of tedious posing. The basket would fetch a few pence and the art supplies it contained, if he found a buyer, were worth at least a half guinea. She sighed. Mama would say she was foolishly trusting, but she could not bring herself to go about suspecting everyone she met of harbouring wicked intentions.

No one with such smiling eyes could possibly turn out to be a rogue. She was not at all surprised to find him waiting outside for her, the loaves sticking out of the basket and the change from the shilling ready in his hand.

The clink of the pennies dropping into her reticule was drowned by the chime of the clock on the church of King Charles the Martyr, striking the half hour.

"It's later than I thought," Polly said, undisturbed. "Mama will wonder where I am. Poor Mama must always have something to worry about."

She herself was not given to anxiety, her only concern at present being that the Russian might not stay long. Wasting no time, she began to plan the portrait as she led him past the theatre and the church, then turned into Cumberland Walk.

The man striding at her side along the high-hedged footpath did not interrupt her musing, though he wondered about its subject. She seemed quite unaware of the impropriety of taking a stranger home with her. Unless, perhaps, she was perfectly aware; perhaps she was looking for a lover?

He frowned at the thought. His experience of England was limited and did not encompass female artists. Certainly she looked respectable, her clothes plain and serviceable, not at all inviting. Her figure was another matter, definitely inviting for the brief moment he had held her in his arms. The memory brought a twinge of desire.

Dunyashka was long ago and very far away.

Though past her first youth, a year or two younger than himself, the Englishwoman was pretty enough, her face round, with pointed chin and straight little nose. Beneath the unfashionable bonnet was a hint of fair hair; her generous mouth was made for kissing — but her eyes, so dark blue as to verge on violet, had held no hint of flirtatiousness. On the contrary, when he first saw her descending the steps they had been focussed on some inner vision. He had seen her momentarily alarmed when she fell, then eager at the prospect of painting him, then amused, yet on the whole it was her serenity that impressed him.

He stole a glance at her sideways. At

present the inner vision held sway. She seemed utterly untroubled by the possibility that her mother might object to her bringing home a ragged stranger.

At the least, this encounter should prove interesting.

She stopped at a wooden gate in the hedge. He read the words "The Crow's Nest" carved in the upper crosspiece.

"Here we are." She opened the gate.

The walled garden beyond was a manifestation of solid respectability. A brick path wound uphill between neat rows of cabbages and Brussels sprouts, daffodils and crocus blooming beneath a pair of fruit trees, a strip of close-clipped lawn with colourful flowerbeds on either side. A delicate fragrance wafted to meet them as they climbed the slope towards the narrow terrace house at the top.

"Wallflowers," she said, taking a deep breath of the scented air. "Cream and yellow and orange and scarlet and crimson. I have tried painting them, but on canvas the hues are startling, even clashing."

"Better in reality than in picture, like beautiful woman." He infused his tone with warm admiration.

Most females would have justifiably accepted his words as a compliment. She appeared to regard it as a philosophical statement.

"Sometimes I wonder whether a picture can ever be more than a poor substitute for reality," she responded thoughtfully. "It may serve as a reminder, or to point out some aspect . . . but you will not care to hear me rattle on about my favourite subject when you are hungry! You shall eat at once."

They had reached the house. Following her up the three steps to the back door he took her elbow. She glanced back at him over her shoulder, laughing, and said, "I do not make a practice of falling down stairs, you know."

"But I make practice of assisting pretty girls on stairs." This time she could not mistake his meaning. She gave him a dubious look and turned away to open the door.

From a narrow, dark corridor they stepped into a cosy kitchen hung with gleaming copper pans and plaited strings of onions. He set the basket on the well-scrubbed table.

"Polly!"

The woman standing in the doorway, dressed in black bombazine, was small and angular and scandalised.

"Polly, who is this? Whatever can you be

17

thinking of to bring a strange man home with you! Who is he?"

He performed his most elegant bow. "Allow me to present self, *madame*. I am Nikolai Mikhailovich Volkov." Remembering the trouble the English always had with Russian names, he added, "Or Kolya, is more easy."

"A foreigner!" Her voice rose to a horrified squeak.

"Kolya is from Russia, Mama. He saved me from a nasty fall. I might have broken my leg."

"Polly!"

"My limb," she amended. "I brought him home because I want to paint him."

"That is not reason enough to be taking in vagabonds off the street. Give him a half crown and send him on his way."

Her daughter ignored this sage advice. She turned to Kolya. "I never thought to tell you my name. I am Mary Howard, known to my family as Polly, as you heard, and this is my mother, Mrs. Howard."

Again he bowed. He wondered what she would say if he addressed her as Polly. She might not even notice, but her mother certainly would. When she called him Kolya, she made plain her opinion of his low status — English custom was no different from

Russian in that regard. Looking down at his clothes, his splitting boots and calloused hands, he could not blame her.

Polly was so nearly a Russian name — Polya, for Pelageya, his oldest sister's little girl's name. He would address her as Miss Howard, but he would think of her as Polly.

"Kolya is hungry, Mama. What can we give him to eat?"

To his amusement, the appeal to practicality calmed the older woman. She began to unload the basket while Polly took off her bonnet, revealing neat braids piled in honey-blonde coils.

"Polly, you are not wearing your cap and your pelisse is soiled. It looks as if you have been kneeling in the street! What will people think? And where are the eggs I asked you to buy? There is nothing under the bread but your oddments."

"Eggs? I knew there was something else. How lucky that I did not buy them. They would have broken when I fell." She took a sketch pad and a piece of charcoal from the pile on the table, sat down, and began to draw.

"You will have to make do with cheese, Kolya, and there is some oxtail soup I can heat for you. Sit down, sit down. Cut yourself some bread."

19

"Thank you, *madame,* you are very kind."

Mrs. Howard heaved a long-suffering sigh. "It is a waste of breath to argue with my daughter." She bustled off to the larder.

Kolya took a seat at the table. "You are drawing me already, Miss Howard? You wish that I sit very still?"

"No, not yet. I find that portraits have more life if I do a number of unposed sketches of my subject first. Pray go ahead and eat and when you are done, if you do not object, I should be glad to hear how you come to be in England."

"Yes, indeed," seconded Mrs. Howard, looking at him askance as she set a cheese and a dish of cold meat before him. Her suspicion was unabated, though it had no apparent effect on the extent of her hospitality. "I trust you have no objection to explaining what you are doing so far from home, young man."

Polly laughed. "Really, Mama, no one would guess you were married to a sailor," she said affectionately. "Do you suppose Papa had to submit to interrogation every time he set foot on a foreign shore?"

"Are you a sailor?" she demanded.

"No, *madame,* but I was a soldier."

20

"And the Russians were our allies," Polly pointed out. "Did you fight Napoleon, Kolya?"

"At Borodino and at Waterloo."

"At Waterloo?" For the first time, Mrs. Howard looked on him with something approaching approval. "Take more bread, Kolya. Your soup will be ready in a trice."

As he ate, he wondered just how much to tell the Howards. It was his opportunity to raise himself in Polly's estimation, yet it seemed likely that they would simply dismiss his story as a tall tale, as unwarrantable boasting. He did not want to figure in her eyes as a braggart.

The beginning of his flight had been dramatic enough, before it dwindled into a struggle for existence. He recalled the warning in the night, the mad dash across the snowy plain in his troika, until the lead horse foundered. Riding bareback he had crossed the Polish frontier just ahead of his pursuers. Though most of Poland had been forcibly incorporated into Russia in 1814, he had friends there more than willing to thwart the tsar by hiding him.

Yes, it would make a good story, if he chose to tell it.

The decision was postponed. He had just finished eating the rich, meaty soup when a

21

mob-capped head appeared around the door. "Carter's brung the packing cases, madam. Where d'you want 'em set?"

"There's the china in the dining room, Ella, and linen upstairs, and all sorts of bits and pieces in the parlour, besides the kitchen goods. Oh, and Miss Polly's things in the attic. Did he bring the special boxes for her paintings?"

"Yes'm, I asked." The maid nodded, greying curls bobbing.

"I had best come and direct him myself. Polly, you cannot possibly start on a portrait now. There is far too much to be done."

"Botheration!" said Miss Howard. "I quite forgot."

2

Kolya set about packing china in straw as efficiently as if he had spent his entire life at it. He knelt on the floor and Polly, admiring his deft motions, passed him plate after plate of her mother's best Wedgwood from the old Welsh dresser.

"It is kind in you to offer to help," she said. "You have completely won over Mama."

"Even Russian vagabond is good for something," he said with a grin that made her fingers itch for a piece of charcoal. "*Madame* will not now demand story of my life, I think?"

"I daresay you will think me shockingly inquisitive, but I still would like to know why you are in England, if you do not mind telling."

"I do not mind." He sat back on his heels with a sigh. "I have made tsar very angry. Tsar — that is our emperor, you understand."

"The Emperor Alexander? Who was here

23

in 1814 for the peace celebrations?" She wondered what he had done to enrage the monarch.

"*Da*. I too was here, as one of Imperial Majesty's soldiers. I admire greatly your country, and have English friends. When was forced to leave Russia, decided to come here. Is long way, and I had very little money with me. I worked for food in Poland, in Germany; begged to ride on carts of farmers. In Holland, found place as sailor on English fishing boat."

"So you are a sailor, as well as a soldier. That will please Mama."

Shaking his head, he said wryly, "Am not good sailor. When we come to harbour at Rye, captain will not pay me."

Polly was indignant. "How dare he!"

"He said food I ate is worth more than I have earned. So now I walk to London to find my friends. Is not difficult to find work for meal. Here, as I cannot be good dog and sit for food, will help with packing instead." Suiting action to the word, he returned to the task. Polly handed him a soup tureen. "Now is your turn, Miss Howard. You tell me why we pack household goods in box for carter."

"We are going to live with my brother Ned." Polly explained that Ned was a land agent. After several years learning the business, he had spent the past three years restoring a much neglected estate for his employer. At last he had a house fit to invite his family to join him. "He is coming to fetch us tomorrow," she added.

"You were not pleased when *matyushka* — mother — reminded you," Kolya observed. "You are not happy to go to brother?"

"Oh yes, Ned is a dear. I was just disappointed not to have the chance to paint you." Forgetting the pile of saucers she had just picked up, she thought of the sketches she had already made. Had she managed to catch his lively expression, the amusement in those extraordinary eyes? "I believe I have enough already to produce a tolerable likeness, though it will not be as good as if I could paint from life."

He stood up and removed the saucers from her hands. "You paint always portraits?"

"I like landscapes best. That is another reason I'm pleased to be removing to Loxwood — there will be different scenes to paint. I have lived all my life in Tunbridge Wells, you know. You will scarcely believe that, except for going to Penshurst Place and Chiddingstone to see the art collections, I have never been farther afield than Tonbridge."

"You have never left this town? Pass cups, if you please, Miss Howard."

She complied. "Oh, Tonbridge is a quite separate town, spelled differently though it sounds the same. It is four or five miles north of here, and it has a ruined castle which I love to paint. Loxwood is forty miles off."

"Is great distance." His voice was grave, but his eyes laughed at her.

"It's all very well for you to tease, who have travelled so far. To me it is a great distance."

"Perhaps you must leave sweetheart?"

"No, there is only the rector, and Mr. Grant, who is a schoolmaster in Tonbridge, and Dr. Leacroft. I do not care . . ." But what on earth was she doing discussing her oft-rejected suitors with a stranger? "No, no sweetheart," she said firmly. "And you, did you leave someone in Russia?"

He sighed. "Parents, brothers, sisters. My poor *matyushka* wept when I left. Perhaps we never see each other again. She gave me icon to watch over me." From beneath his homespun shirt he pulled a silver medallion with a painted face, on a silver chain. "*Svyatoy Nikolai,* Saint Nicholas, my namesake and patron saint of travellers. And of Holy Russia."

As Polly leaned down to see the icon better, he put it reverently to his lips and kissed it. The eyes he raised to her face, however, were anything but reverent. Polly felt herself blush and hastily straightened.

Unused to being put to the blush, she was cross. Even Dr. Leacroft's enthusiastic, and sometimes indecorously anatomical, compliments had always failed to disconcert her, let alone to make her feel as peculiar inside as she now felt at the gleam in Kolya's eyes. She was inclined to think she had better call Mama to supervise the packing of the silver while she went up to her attic studio to sort out her canvases.

But Kolya was now carefully stuffing straw between the nested cups. Had she imagined that warm look, the look that had seemed to tell her that the saint's image was a poor substitute for her lips?

A vigorous rat-a-tat-tat at the front door interrupted her confused thoughts.

"Polly," her mother called from above-stairs, "pray see who is there."

Before she reached the dining-room door, she heard the front door open with a crash, followed by a thunderous tread that suggested the presence of a stampeding herd of cart-horses.

"Nicky? Surely not!" She hurried into the hall, where a sturdy, fair-haired youth seized her in a bear hug, lifting her feet from the floor. "Nicky! Put me down at once."

"Not unless you promise to stop calling me Nicky, Poll. I'm not a child anymore."

"I promise, I promise. But what are you doing here in the middle of term, Master Nicholas?"

"Nick will do," he said jauntily.

Polly put her hands on her hips and scowled at her fifteen-year-old brother. "Don't try to avoid the question."

"Nicky! My dear boy!" Mrs. Howard pattered down the stairs and embraced her son. "Why have they sent you home?" she asked anxiously. "Are you ill?"

"Well, not exactly, Mama." Gently but firmly Nick extricated himself from her clinging arms. "Is there anything to eat? I'm half starved."

"Yes, of course, my poor boy. Come into the kitchen."

Polly put out a restraining hand. "Wait just a minute. He is not likely to expire from hunger. Let us have an explanation first."

"It was a famous jape, Polly," he assured her ingenuously. "You would have laughed yourself silly, honestly."

"Nicholas Howard, cut line."

Nick looked wildly round for an escape and saw Kolya, leaning in the dining-room doorway. "Who's that?"

"Kolya. He is helping with the packing. Now . . ."

"Packing? Damn — dash it, I forgot all about it. When are we going to Loxwood? It's deuced lucky I didn't come back and find everybody gone."

"It would have served you right," said his unsympathetic sister. "What was a famous jape?"

"Oh Nicky, what have you done?" wailed his mother.

No further delaying tactics came to mind. "We — that's Greville and I — we borrowed a dancing bear from a Gypsy and hid it in the vestry. Old Bagwig went in there to put on his cassock for morning chapel. He came out backwards like a cork from a bottle with the bear following him. Half the fellows jumped up on the pews and hopped around squealing, as if that would have saved them from anything bigger than a mouse," Nicholas said scornfully. "The other half gathered around poor old Bruin and flapped their prayer books at him as if they were trying to stop him, but really egging him on. Greville and I were waiting in the gallery above the door with a sheet to drop over the bear when it passed below, but the sheet landed on Bagwig by mistake. I think he thought the bear had got him. You should have heard him yell!"

"I'm very glad I did not," Polly said, not quite truthfully.

"Oh, Nicky," moaned Mrs. Howard.

"The bear went blundering past and out of the chapel, where the Gypsy was waiting for it. He rushed it off quick as winking, I can tell you."

"And then?" Polly demanded.

Nick had the grace to look abashed. "Well, the long and the short of it is, I was expelled."

Mrs. Howard burst into tears. "Nicky, how could you!"

"Don't take on so, Ma. I don't care above half . . ."

"When your brother has so generously paid your fees!"

"That's it, though. Why should Ned be wasting his money on school fees when all I want is to go to sea?"

"Do stop arguing, you wretched boy. Hush, Mama," Polly soothed her afflicted parent. "Come and sit down. Ella shall make you a cup of tea and you will feel better in a trice."

"But . . ." Nick began again.

"In Russia," Kolya intervened, "we hunt bears."

Polly flashed him a look of gratitude over her mother's head as Nick turned to him with eager questions.

She took Mrs. Howard into the parlour, where empty crates awaited the souvenirs of Captain Howard's voyages. Carved masks from Africa hung above the chintz-covered chairs and a glass-fronted cabinet displayed a Chinese jade Buddha, a feathered Red Indian peace pipe, strange shells from the South Seas, and a jaguar carved in stone. As Polly now pointed out, her father had circumnavigated the globe several times in the course of thirty years at sea, and in the end had succumbed to sickness, not drowning. There was no reason to suppose that Nick would fare worse.

Ella appeared with the promised tea, which further soothed the distraught mother. A judicious reminder that Nick was hungry, and that there was a great deal of work to be done if they were to be ready for Ned on the morrow, completed the cure.

"Ned will know what to do," sniffed Mrs. Howard dolefully. "He is such a reliable boy. And I must say, Polly, that *sometimes* you are a great comfort to me. I shall fry up some potatoes for Nicky, to go with the rest of the cold mutton."

She bustled off to the kitchen, and Polly returned to the dining room. Her brother and the Russian were on their knees, packing straw into the full china crate.

"So I shot my poor horse and left him to wolves," Kolya was saying, "and while they were eating, I stumbled through snow to peasant's *izba* — hut, I think is word."

"Polly, Kolya has had the most amazing adventures!" Nick informed her. Kolya nudged him in the ribs. "Oh yes, I'm sorry I upset Mama. I expect I ought to have told you privately and let you break the news. But what was a fellow to do when you kept asking why I was home?"

Avoiding this invitation to dispute, she said, "Go and apologize to Mama. She is in the kitchen . . ."

"Food!" Nick jumped up and sped from the room.

"Thank you for diverting him," Polly said, dropping into a chair. "He is at an argumentative age, I fear."

"Hungry age, also. Is good lad, I think?"

"He's a dear, though it was monstrous wicked of him to introduce a bear into the church." Involuntarily she giggled. "All the same, I wish I could have seen it. Pray don't

32

tell Nick I said so."

"Was famous jape indeed. Expelled means he cannot return to school?"

"Yes. Ned will be distressed, I fear, but I'm not really surprised. Nick is not at all inclined to book-learning. In fact, he has wanted to join the Navy, like Papa, since he was in leading strings. Mama dislikes the notion — Papa was away so much and she missed him dreadfully. And Ned always wanted to go to university, but there was not enough money for a good school, so he felt he was doing Nick a good turn by sending him to Winchester."

"I understand. Is not always easy to know how best to help others. To get good position on ship for Nick, this is possible?"

"He cannot go as a common seaman, of course. Papa started out as a midshipman, so I expect that is what Nick wants. It is the lowest grade of commissioned officer. Ned will know how to go about it."

Kolya nodded and stood up. "Box is full. Is necessary to nail top, or tie with rope?"

"I shall ask Ella." Polly wondered why she had explained about Nick's schooling. It was nothing to do with the stranger, and he could not possibly be interested. Somehow it was difficult to remember that he was a stranger. Suddenly recalling her disconcerting reaction when he kissed the icon, she said abruptly, "Thank you for the work you have done. Since Nick is come, he can help with the rest. I shall give you money for the stage fare to London, and enough for a night's lodging in case you cannot find your friends at once."

"I am not beggar." His response was unexpectedly sharp. "I have earned meal, no more. If you do not need me, I shall be on my way."

"But it is too far to walk. London is thirty miles and more."

Once more he was amused, her unintended insult seemingly forgiven. "I have walked much farther, Miss Howard. Since you have not time for painting, is best I go."

Between the way he flustered her and the upset of Nick's arrival, Polly had forgotten the portrait. Kolya's reminder re-awoke her enthusiasm. "No, stay. With you and Nick to help, the packing will be done much faster. And with Nick here, there can be no objection if you spend the night. I shall be able at least to start the portrait tomorrow. Please?"

He looked doubtful. "To start portrait will be useful?"

"Yes, oh yes. I can draw the right pose on the canvas, and work out the colour tones.

And you will earn several more meals so that when you leave you will be rested and well fed."

"How can I resist? Very well, I shall be good dog and sit for food, if *matyushka* agrees."

"Mama will agree," said Polly blithely. And when Ned comes tomorrow, she thought, perhaps he will be able to persuade the proud Russian to accept the fare to London.

3

"And the story you told Nick about the wolves, was that true?"

"Almost." Kolya was sitting patiently on a stool under the skylight Captain Howard had had set in the roof when he came home and found his daughter seriously interested in painting. "It happened to friend, not to me. When wolves chased me, I was not so brave. I hid up tree."

"I cannot tell whether to believe you or not."

A cry of anguish rang up the stairs. "Polly! *Polly!*"

"What is it, Mama? I cannot come just now." She was preparing the colour for Kolya's hair and she had it almost right. Just a tiny spot more of the yellow ochre — once she had a sample on a scrap of canvas she could match it when she came to paint the portrait, when he was gone. Mrs. Howard's footsteps were heard pattering up the stairs to the attic at a rapid pace. She trotted in, slightly out of breath.

"Polly! You never posted the letter to Ned. Ella moved your chest of drawers to sweep underneath and she found it lying there. You drew a picture on it!"

"Oh, yes, I remember. The sealing wax looked like a rose so I drew some leaves around it. My window was open so it must have blown onto the floor while I was putting on my bonnet, and I forgot it. I'm sorry, Mama. Kolya, sit down, pray. The light changes when you stand."

He had politely risen when Mrs. Howard entered, and he was buttoning his shirt. Art outweighing embarrassment, Polly had had him open it at the throat to display his icon.

Her mother was far too agitated to notice this impropriety. "How can you be so calm? What are we to do if Ned does not come today? The tenants are moving in to-morrow, and even if they can be put off, the carter has taken everything but what we need for one night. Oh Polly, how could you?"

"But it was only a confirmation, was it not? Ned himself set the date in the first place. You can rely on Ned."

"Ma?" The house shook as Nick thundered up the stairs. "There you are. What else is there to eat?"

"Nothing beyond your brother's dinner,

though I daresay he will not be here to eat it. And do not call me Ma in that odiously vulgar way."

"I beg your pardon, Mother dear, but you keep calling me Nicky and I've asked you not to a thousand times. Polly, did you know that Kolya's real name is Nikolai, which is the Russian for Nicholas? Is it not famous?"

"Famous," said his sister dryly, testing the colour she had mixed. "I suppose you will next want us to call you Kolya."

"Lord no, Nick will do. Mother, I'm *starving*. When's dinner-time?"

"When Ned arrives, if he does." Mrs. Howard cast a reproachful glance at Polly. "Polly, you have paint on your chin."

She dabbed at her chin with a corner of her smock. "I shall wash it off later."

"But I can't wait," Nick insisted.

"I'm sure Ned never had such an appetite at your age. You will have to go down to the shops and buy something to eat now and some extra eggs for breakfast."

"Ho, not I. Marketing is for females."

Kolya laughed. "Is plain to see you do not understand meaning of 'starving,' Master Nicholas. I will go to shops for *madame,* if she wishes, as soon as Miss Howard is finished."

"Oh, if you are going, I'll go, too," said Nick at once. "How long are you going to be, Poll?"

"Ten minutes. The best of the light is nearly gone and I have everything I need." She thinned the mixture of pigments on her palette with a drop of turpentine and tested the colour again.

The aromatic odour reminded her all too clearly of the moment when she had made Kolya's acquaintance by falling into his arms. His gentle strength, his kindness, his willingness to help, and his lively sense of humour, all added up to a man who was far too attractive for comfort. It was just as well that tomorrow he would be on his way. She did not even know for what dastardly deed he had been exiled, she reminded herself.

She looked up to find that her mother and Nick had gone. If Mama knew how she felt, she would never have left her alone with Kolya. Of course, to Mrs. Howard it was inconceivable that her well-brought-up daughter might be attracted to a common tramp, however gentlemanly his manners and laughing his eyes.

His eyes were not laughing at present. He was regarding her with an intentness that made her cheeks feel hot. She hoped he did not notice her flush — the light in the attic had dimmed suddenly as the setting sun passed behind a cloud.

"That is all," she said quickly, busying herself with cleaning her brushes. "Thank you for your patience."

"May I see?"

"No, there is nothing to see as yet."

"Then I go remove Master Nicholas from under feet of *matyushka*."

It was not only herself whom he had won over, thought Polly, consoled, as he went off. Nick was halfway to hero worship; Mama had no qualms about giving Kolya the run of the house; and after eating with him in the kitchen last night, Ella had reported that he was a "right neighbourly sort," her highest accolade.

As she washed her brushes and palette and took off the cotton smock with its multicoloured spots and smears, Polly wondered what Ned would think of the stranger his family had taken in. Kolya's charm would not easily overcome her conscientious older brother's sense of propriety.

Above all, Ned was wholly reliable. Polly was not in the least surprised when he arrived half an hour later, to be greeted by a tearful welcome from his relieved mother.

"But of course I am here," he said, puzzled, as he kissed her cheek. "We fixed the date a good fortnight since."

"I feared you might not remember."

"I told you that you might rely on him," said Polly, coming down the stairs. "Let me take your coat, Ned. You see, Mama wrote to remind you and I forgot to post the letter."

His eyes met hers in a glance of comprehension, and he chuckled. "Polly, my dear, if the house burned down you would stand there studying the shape and colour of the flames and forget to notify the fire brigade."

Though he was five years her elder, the brother and sister understood each other well. Mr. Edward Howard was a kindly man who had learned long ago to make allowances for Polly's overmastering passion — when he discovered that his remonstrances had no effect whatsoever. In looks he took after their father, sturdily built, like Nick, but with dark brown hair and grey eyes. His dark blue coat, buckskin breeches, and plain necktie were neat and respectable, making no effort to ape the fashions of his betters.

He hugged Polly. "You are looking very well."

"Polly, you still have paint on your chin," Mrs. Howard said, adding anxiously, "Come and sit down, Ned, dear. You must be fatigued after your journey."

"Not at all," he assured her, following her into the parlour. The room looked bare without the African masks on the walls. "Lord John lent me one of his Grace's travelling carriages and a groom to drive it, so you shall go to your new home in fine style tomorrow." He sat down with a sigh of satisfaction. "How pleasant it will be to have my family about me after all these years."

The slam of the back door and an eager, earthshaking tread in the hall announced the return of the shoppers.

"Rather more of the family than you expected," said Polly dryly as Nick burst into the room.

"Ned! The ostler at the Sussex told me you'd driven up in a fancy rig, so I went to take a look. Is it the duke's? It's bang up to the nines!"

"Yes, it's the duke's. What the deuce are you doing here, Nicholas?"

"I've been shopping for Mother," said Nick nonchalantly, but there was a wary look in his eye.

"Did you buy everything on the list?" Mrs. Howard asked.

"Yes, Kolya is putting it in the kitchen. Ned, you must meet Kolya. He's from Russia and he's had the most famous adventures." He turned and yelled down the hall, "Kolya, come and meet my brother."

Polly leaned close to Ned's ear and whispered, "Nick deserves a thundering scold, but I beg you will not rake him over the coals in Mama's presence. She is upset enough already. And I shall explain later about . . ."

"Ned, this is Kolya. Polly is painting him."

The Russian stood in the doorway, tall and straight. Despite his shabbiness, there was nothing subservient about him. His elegant bow seemed more appropriate to a greeting from gentleman to gentleman.

Ned nodded in return and murmured to Polly, "If you are painting him, I daresay there is no need to ask for further explanation!"

"Kolya is going to London to find his friends," Polly said aloud. "I offered him money for the stage fare, but he refused it."

"Very proper," Ned approved. "In which part of London do your friends reside, Kolya?"

Kolya moved forward with easy grace. Polly thought he was about to take a seat, but at the last moment he recollected his position.

"I shall go first to Stafford House, sir. I

made acquaintance of duke's son, Lord John Danville, in 1814 and met him again in St Petersburg last year."

"Lord John! That is flying high. I fear you will be disappointed, for Lord John is presently residing at Five Oaks."

"Five Oaks? I think I have heard him mention. Is country estate of duke, *nyet?* Is far from London?"

"Five Oaks is near Loxwood, is it not?" Polly eagerly asked her brother.

"The estates adjoin," he admitted with obvious reluctance. "His Grace bought Loxwood Manor from a neighbour. It is to be Lord John's as soon as the house is refurbished."

"The Duke of Stafford is Ned's employer," Polly explained to Kolya. "We can take you there tomorrow. If Lord John cannot help you, you will be no farther from London, will he, Ned?"

"It is roughly the same distance, to be sure, but I cannot like to be responsible . . ."

"Lord John will help me." Kolya's voice rang with absolute certainty.

Ned was still dubious. Thoughts of blackmail flitted through his mind. He knew that Lord John had met with difficulties, even danger, in Russia and had been desperately ill on his return to England. After several months of convalescence he had married, and he and his young bride were spending their honeymoon at Five Oaks. Even if this stranger were perfectly honest, the young couple would hardly welcome an intruder at this time.

"But is not my wish to cause trouble," the Russian continued. "I can walk to Five Oaks as well as to London."

"It will not be any trouble!" Nick declared. The lad had been amazingly — or perhaps prudently — silent for some time. "Kolya can stand up behind like a footman and I shall ride on the box with the coachman."

"Oh no, Nicky, that is by far too dangerous," Mrs. Howard said at once, but to Ned's surprise she went on, "Indeed, I can see no harm in taking Kolya with us."

Now how had the fellow managed to ingratiate himself with their ever-cautious mother?

"He really deserves some reward," Polly added persuasively. "He saved me, you know, when I fell down the steps from the Pantiles. I was thinking about painting and did not watch my step. Mr. Irving had just given me the money for the pictures he sold for me this past quarter."

"Ned, I wish you will stop your sister

selling her pictures," begged his mother. "It is not at all genteel."

"I think it's famous," said Nick loyally. "I hope you make pots of money, Poll."

Ned was torn. It distressed him that Polly felt the need of earning money, but the supplement to his own salary and Mrs. Howard's meager jointure was most welcome. She had also managed to set aside a small nest egg for herself, he knew, which was a relief as he was in no position to provide for her.

Besides, she would not stop simply because he told her to. "Congratulations, Polly," he said. "Did Mr. Irving sell many for you?"

"He sells all the views of this area that I paint: the Pantiles, the Common, even the ruins of Tonbridge Castle. Many of the visitors to the Chalybeate Spring want a memento of their stay."

"Is good people are willing to pay for your work, Miss Howard," the Russian said quietly. "Thus, you know is of value to others, *nyet?*"

"Yes! Yes, that is just how I feel." Polly favoured the stranger with a delighted smile, and Ned realised that he had failed to understand his sister's pride in her art. It was not money she cared about, but recognition. She turned back to him. "Do you think there is a shop near Loxwood that will take my pictures?"

Ned hated to disappoint her. "You might find one in Horsham. It's a pretty town and the assizes are held there, so there are plenty of visitors at times."

"I doubt lawyers and prisoners will want keepsakes of the place," she said with a sigh.

"They will if they win their cases," Nick encouraged her. "You should paint pictures of the gaol to remind them of what they have escaped."

Polly laughed. "It is worth trying. Is Horsham on the way to Loxwood, Ned? Shall we pass through it?"

"Yes, you will see it tomorrow. If we make good time, we might stop there for luncheon, though I left the duke's horses in Crawley."

"Lord John lent you his cattle, too?" Nick was thrilled. "I wager they are famous bits of blood and bone. Lord John must be a regular Trojan."

"Is good fellow," Kolya confirmed.

Ned found himself the target of four pairs of eyes.

"Well?" demanded Nick. "Are we taking Kolya?"

If the man was going to walk to Five Oaks

47

anyway he might as well go with them. After all, there were plenty of servants there to deal with an encroaching foreigner if necessary. Ned sighed and gave in. "Very well, we shall take you up, Kolya."

"Thank you, sir."

"And you," Ned said severely to his young brother, "come up to my room with me while I wash. I've a bone to pick with you."

It was unfortunate, as he confessed to Polly later, that Nick's bear story made him laugh. After that it was impossible to instill a proper sense of wrongdoing in the boy, let alone to discipline him thoroughly.

"I could not help remembering," he told her as they climbed the stairs to bed, "that you warned me an academic career would not suit him. However, he has picked up some little learning at least, and now I shall just have to see what I can do to help him join the Navy."

"I hope he realizes how lucky he is to have such an amiable brother," said Polly, kissing him good-night.

He hugged her. Despite her vagaries, she was a dear girl, and he was glad that at last he was able to have her and his mother to live with him. He had worked very hard for this moment. Even Nick's misdeeds could not spoil it. He just hoped Lord John would not be too infuriated by his delivery of that wretched foreigner his impulsive sister had taken under her wing.

4

In the morning, Ned had to admit that both Nick and Kolya were a great help when it came to packing up the last of the household goods and loading the coach. It did not take long — fortunately Mrs. Howard had let her house furnished, and owing to her efficiency almost all the moveables had gone with the carter.

Everything was ready. Mrs. Howard locked the door and was about to give Ella the key to take to the neighbour's when suddenly she stopped and looked round.

"Polly! Where has the girl got to now? Nicholas, have you seen her?"

"Not since breakfast. Ned, do say I may ride on the box."

"Polly went up to the attic half an hour ago," Ned said, "to make sure she had not left anything in her studio. Perhaps she is still up there, lost in one of her dreams."

Kolya laughed. "I wager Miss Howard is sketching in garden." He held out his hand. "Give key, please. I fetch."

Mrs. Howard gave him the key and he went back into the house. Ned looked at his mother with a frown. "How does the fellow know so much about my sister?"

"He's not stupid," Nick answered with unexpected indignation. "It only takes an hour or two to discover Polly's crazy about art. Mother, you don't mind if I ride on the box, do you?"

"Oh dear, do you think it safe, Ned?"

Once Ned had reassured his mother as to the safety of riding with the groom, he found it difficult to punish Nick for his misbehaviour at school by forbidding it. While he was humming and hawing, Kolya returned with Polly, sketch book in hand.

"I did not realize you were waiting," she apologized. "The clouds are so extraordinary I wanted to draw them before they blow away. They look like a ploughed field."

Everyone immediately stared at the sky. The clouds did indeed look as if they had been raked into neat rows. Lit from below by the rising sun, they shone pearly gold. A momentary feeling of awe filled Ned, and he turned to thank Polly for drawing his attention to the sight.

Kolya was before him. *"Prekrasno,"* he murmured. "Beautiful. Is special gift of artist to see what others fail to notice. Thank you, Miss Howard."

Polly smiled at him. Dash it, thought Ned, annoyed, the Russian said it better than he could have himself. He busied himself handing his mother and sister into the carriage while Kolya took his place on the narrow perch behind intended for footmen.

Taking advantage of his distraction, Nick climbed up onto the box. As Ned followed Ella inside, to sit beside the maid with his back to the horses, he consoled himself with the thought that there was more room, and definitely more peace, without his brother.

No sooner did they leave the town behind them to roll along the open road than Nick's voice floated back in an urgent plea to "spring 'em." Mrs. Howard looked alarmed, but as the duke's groom paid her importunate son no heed, she soon settled down on the luxuriously padded seat. The carriage was so well sprung that she dozed for much of the way. Polly, meanwhile, gazed out of the open window, far too entranced by the new sights to care about the layer of road dust deposited upon her person.

When they stopped for luncheon in Horsham, Polly once again disappeared.

This time she returned before anyone went to look for her.

"I found a bookseller," she reported happily. "He has promised to display two pictures of the town or the surrounding countryside, and if they sell quickly he will take more."

Mrs. Howard sighed heavily. Ned knew she had hoped that the removal from Tunbridge Wells would put an end to her daughter's commercial ventures. He half sympathized, but Polly was so delighted it was impossible not to be pleased for her.

They reached Loxwood in the middle of the afternoon. A quarter mile beyond the gates of Loxwood Manor, they turned from the narrow lane into one even narrower, on the outskirts of the village. The house the duke had provided for his bailiff stood on the corner. The carriage pulled up on the strip of gravel separating the whitewashed, tile-roofed building from the lane.

Ned stepped out and handed down his mother and sister. "Welcome home," he said.

"This is it?" whooped Nick, scrambling down from the box.

Polly squeezed Ned's hand. "I know we are going to be very happy here. I cannot wait to unpack my paints."

The front door swung open and his elderly cook-housekeeper appeared, neat and respectable in her black dress and white apron. She was accompanied by a mouth-watering smell of baking.

"Mother, this is Mrs. Coates. She will do all the cooking and marketing so you shall be a lady of leisure and drink tea with the vicar's wife."

Hung with oddments of baggage, Ella emerged from the carriage and regarded her fellow servant with a glowering face. "Since you won't be needing me no more, madam, I'll just turn meself around and go right back to Tunbridge Wells."

"Oh dear," said Mrs. Howard. "Indeed I cannot manage without you, Ella."

Ned hurried to excuse himself. "I'll have to leave you to make the peace, Mother. I left my horse at Five Oaks yesterday, so I must go back with the carriage as soon as we have unloaded the luggage. Do you go in and settle yourselves, and I shall return in no time."

"You need not worry about Ella and Mrs. Coates," Polly whispered, "for it is exactly the sort of problem Mama enjoys worrying about. If Lord John will not help Kolya, will you bring him back here?"

He looked at her in surprise. "No, Polly, I

54

will not. It would not be at all proper."

"Just for a few days, until I finish the portrait."

"I'm sure Kolya himself had rather go on to London to find his other friends," he said gently, concerned at his usually cheerful sister's despondency. "You will not wish to delay him further."

She sighed. "I suppose not. But you must make him take this money. He is more like to take it from you than from a female, surely." She pressed three sovereigns into his hand.

Ned did not know what to say, so he was glad when at that moment Mrs. Howard called Polly into the house.

Kolya had just helped Nick carry in one of the trunks. Polly met him coming out, and Ned saw them exchanging a few words. However, he was busy giving the groom a hand with the second trunk and did not hear what was said. Soon everything was unloaded. Kolya joined the groom on the box and they set off again.

Cross-country Five Oaks was no distance, but by the winding lanes it was a good six miles. Ned had plenty of time to wonder how Lord John would feel about the appearance of an out-at-elbows foreigner claiming to be his friend. By the time the carriage rumbled into the stable yard of the duke's vast mansion, he was decidedly apprehensive.

While the carriage horses were unharnessed, the head groom sent one of his underlings to saddle Ned's hack for him, another to the house to report the Russian's arrival.

The horse beat Lord John by a short head. Ned was just taking the reins from a stable boy when his lordship strode into the yard and looked around.

"Kolya? Kolya, my dear fellow, it really is you!"

The Russian flung his arms around Lord John and kissed him on both cheeks. His lordship fervently returned the embrace, to the fascination of Ned and the stable hands. This display was followed by some back slapping, both men talking at once in an incoherent babble.

As surprised as he was relieved by Kolya's welcome, Ned wanted to be on his way. However, he felt that as his lordship had come out, he ought to stay and thank him for the loan of the carriage. Unable to get a word in edgewise, he was about to give up when Lord John said, "But you must come into the house at once, Kolya. Beckie won't thank me for keeping you from her."

"So you marry Rebecca Ivanovna? Congratulations, my dear John. Am very delighted. One moment, if you please." He turned to Ned. "Must thank you, sir, for courtesy and assistance to unknown traveller."

He held out his hand and Ned, bemused, shook it. "It was nothing," he said awkwardly.

"Howard brought you?" asked Lord John. "My thanks, Howard. Her ladyship and I shan't forget this."

"I'm happy to be of service, my lord. And I must thank you for lending me the carriage."

"Family arrived all right and tight, are they? Splendid. Come on, old chap, we mustn't keep Beckie waiting."

Ned watched them walk away, once again talking nineteen to the dozen. The Russian looked thinner and shabbier than ever beside the strongly built, fashionably dressed English lord.

Pulling on his gloves, he recalled the feel of Kolya's rough, hard-skinned hand. As he mounted and turned Chipper's head towards home, he pondered the mystery of the obviously intimate friendship between the Russian labourer and the son of the Duke of Stafford.

As Kolya followed John into the small, comfortably furnished sitting room, a familiar voice asked eagerly, "Is it really him?"

"Yes, love, it's Kolya." John moved aside and his wife hurried forwards, both hands held out.

"Nikolai Mikhailovich, we were so worried about you."

He took her hands, very conscious that his friend was watching their meeting. He had once had a notion to marry Miss Rebecca Nuthall himself. "I am honoured to be subject of your concern, Lady John," he said.

"Lady John! I am still not used to the name. Will you not call me Rebecca Ivanovna as you did before?" Marriage had given the shy girl he had known poise and self-confidence — and an inner glow of happiness which radiated and made her beautiful.

Kolya glanced at John, who nodded, grinning. "There's no harm in private, and even in public people will only think you are a mad Russian."

"This is true, but I mean to become English gentleman."

John eyed his worn, shapeless clothes and roared with laughter.

"Hush, John, do not be so rude," Rebecca scolded. "Come and sit down, Nikolai Mikhailovich, and tell us everything. His Grace heard from Princess Lieven that the tsar found out you helped us escape and exiled you. Our thoughts have been with you constantly."

"Well, not quite constantly," John demurred, dropping a kiss on his bride's cheek as he sat down on the sofa beside her and took her hand.

It was Kolya's turn to laugh. "I hope new-marrieds have better things to think of." He took a seat opposite the loving couple.

Rebecca blushed. Apparently she had not altogether conquered her shyness. "A great deal, anyway," she amended. "I have been longing to thank you for rescuing me from that terrible place." She shivered and John put his arm around her shoulders.

"Please, is better not to think of past. Some day I tell you my adventures and you tell me how you came back to England. Now we talk of future."

"Looking into my crystal ball," said John, "the first thing I foresee is buying you some new clothes."

Rebecca pressed closer to her husband. Kolya wondered whether talk of a crystal ball had reminded her of the time his presence had saved John from an enraged Gypsy. It would be foolish to deny that they were in his debt. He would willingly accept their hospitality, but pride revolted at the thought of taking money.

"I have not feather to fly," he said, pleased with the English idiom despite his troubles. "Will not run up debt with no prospect to pay tailor."

"My purse is yours, my friend. You said that to me once."

Kolya shook his head. "And you did not take advantage. Nor will I. You say 'hang on sleeve,' yes? I will not hang on sleeve."

John looked stubborn, but Rebecca intervened. "There is no need to buy new clothes. If you do not mind, Nikolai Mikhailovich, I can easily have some of John's things altered to fit you, and Lord Danville left some clothes here too, which he will never miss."

"Thank you, Rebecca Ivanovna, I will not refuse this. Truth is, I hate to wear peasant clothes. Will be good to dress as gentleman once more."

"*Not* my new green coat from Weston," John said threateningly.

Rebecca's voice was demure but her eyes danced. "Why, I was just thinking, love, how well it would become *Knyaz Nikolai*."

"No, no, do not call me prince, I beg of you. Is not right for penniless exile to use title." A thoroughly Russian passion rose in Kolya. "English will mock my country, my family. I love them still, though I have put them behind me forever."

"Forever?" asked John, embarrassed as he always was by the Slavic display of emotion. "You don't think the tsar will relent?"

"Forever. Did I not tell you once that *moya dusha* — my soul is English? I will be English gentleman, plain Mr. Volkov. I will find respectable position to earn living. Perhaps duke will help?" he added hopefully.

"Of course his Grace will help," John assured him. "He knows we owe you our lives."

"If you gentlemen will excuse me, I shall go and sort out some clothes for Mr. Volkov, and draft a letter to his Grace for John to copy." Again Rebecca was teasing her husband, Kolya realised. How the timid girl had blossomed in the warmth of his love!

"Beckie was a governess, remember," said John ruefully as they rose. "And she taught me Russian, too. Sometimes she seems to forget I'm not still one of her pupils." He watched her slight figure every step of the way to the door.

Kolya felt a pang of envy. Dunyashka danced through his mind. But his Dunyashenka had doubtless found another protector long since. The merry ballerina's features faded, and in their place appeared Polly's intent face.

She vanished in turn as John interrupted his reverie. "Sit down and tell me what you've been up to all these months, old man."

The back parlour of Ned's house was a pleasant sitting room with dark oak wainscotting below whitewashed walls on which the African masks Polly was unpacking would look very well. Ned had furnished it with comfortable, overstuffed chairs, unlike the elegant Hepplewhite and Sheraton in the drawing room at the front of the house.

When he arrived home from Five Oaks, Polly saw him stable Chipper in the nearest of the outbuildings on the north side of the garden. She opened one of the casement windows wide and leaned out.

What she really wanted to know was how Lord John had received Kolya. What she said was, "The carter is come already. Your house is in chaos, I fear."

"Our house." With a cheerful smile he strode towards her across the lawn. He looked as if a burden had been lifted from his shoulders, and Polly knew he was relieved to be rid of the Russian, one way or another. "Is Mother pleased with it?"

"Excessively. It was kind in the duke to let you take your pick of the furniture at the manor."

"He is refurnishing the place from cellar to attic for Lord John, though there was nothing wrong with the old pieces."

"Mama is delighted with your choice. I must warn you that having two parlours has vastly set her up in her own conceit. Papa's collection has been banished to the sitting room."

"I know she displayed them only out of loyalty to his memory."

"She always squirmed when visitors commented how *interesting* they are. Guess what she means to decorate the drawing room with."

"That's easy. Your pictures, I hope."

"Yes. I'm certain she has always hoped that if she ignored my painting it would go away. Do you think she is becoming reconciled to having an artist for a daughter?"

"I should not count on it if I were you, but at least she is acknowledging that your work has merit. Speaking of reconciliation, is Ella resigned to Mrs. Coates yet?"

"Heavens no, though she has been brought grudgingly to admit that the house is too large for her to cope with by herself. You never told us that it is so much larger than the Tunbridge Wells house."

"I feared Mother might feel that I was belittling her house. There is not so great a difference."

"Two parlours! And Mama is almost as pleased to have two maidservants. Who takes care of the garden? I'm sure you have not time to keep it so neatly."

"Lord John told me to have one of the Loxwood Manor gardeners come over one day a week."

His mention of Lord John gave Polly the opening she had awaited. "Did . . . did you see his lordship just now?"

"Yes, and he was very grateful that I took Kolya to him. It was a great relief, I can tell you."

"He was pleased to see him?" Polly was equally relieved, though for different reasons. She had hated the thought of Kolya's weary walk to London with no certainty of a welcome when he got there.

"Pleased! Ecstatic is the word. They fell into each other's arms, in what I suppose to be the Russian manner. I cannot understand how my lord can be on intimate terms with such a common fellow."

"His manner was not in the least common," said Polly indignantly.

"His clothes, though, and more significant, his hands."

"Yes, I noticed his hands. But he was forced to work his way here from Russia, which would be enough to account for that. He must be a gentleman, after all." She was glad for Kolya's sake that he was able to return to his proper station in life.

"I hope he was not offended by the way we treated him," said Ned uneasily.

"I daresay we shall never see him again." Polly was unable to repress a deep sigh, but her brother was cheered by her words.

"No, probably not. Do come out, Polly, I have something to show you."

Willing to be distracted from her unaccountable depression, she hurried to the back door. Ned had opened it and was waiting for her.

She looked around with interest. The garden was hedged on two sides, with gates leading respectively to the lane and to a pasture where red Sussex cattle grazed. From here the small buildings on the north side were hidden by a row of fruit trees, including a cherry that seemed about to bloom. Polly's eyes gleamed at the prospect of painting it.

Ned offered his arm and led her towards the outbuildings. The first housed Chipper and a light gig.

"That's a potting shed at the far end," Ned said, waving at it. "This one in the middle is what I want to show you." He opened the door.

The single room, some twelve foot by sixteen, was bare but for a stone sink in one corner and several shelves on the wall beside it. The floor was covered with oilcloth and three large windows in the north wall gleamed spotless.

Polly turned to Ned.

"Your studio, madam," he announced.

Tears rose to her eyes as she flung her arms around him. Blinking furiously — she *never* cried — she murmured, "Dearest Ned, you are quite the best brother in the world."

"Thought you'd like it," he said, satisfied.

5

Polly spent the day after the Howards' arrival at Loxwood unpacking her paintings and supplies and arranging them in her new studio. Ned had the Loxwood estate carpenter build a trestle table to her specifications; Mrs. Coates, with a degree of suspicion which made Ella sniff in scorn, was persuaded to give up a pair of old kitchen stools and a bundle of rags; and Mrs. Howard was invited to pick her choice of the pictures she wanted for the drawing room.

As she had never before expressed any interest in Polly's avocation, she was surprised by the variety she had to choose from.

"Why, Polly, some of these are quite charming. I should like the daffodils and the geraniums — such gay colours — and the view from your bedroom window across to the Common. Oh, and here is one of the house. I do hope the tenants are taking care of my house." She had to find something to worry about.

Polly hid a smile. "I'm sure they are, Mama. They had excellent references or Ned would never have let it to them. Is that enough or do you want some more?"

"One more, I think, to go over the fireplace. Gracious, here is one of your poor dear father. I never knew you had painted a portrait of your father or I should have hung it in the house long since."

Her daughter refrained from reminding her that at the time she had been vexed by her husband's insistence on spending so much of his brief leave posing for his portrait.

Though Polly's technique had improved greatly since then, the captain's grey, far-seeing eyes gazed out from the canvas and his weatherbeaten features expressed both geniality and the habit of command. If the gold braid on the hat lying on the table beside him looked somewhat like scrambled egg, and the rigging on the model ship was tied in inextricable knots, Mrs. Howard did not mind. Here was Captain Howard of the Royal Navy, to be proudly displayed to her new acquaintances.

"Thank you, dear," she said. "Ned's carpenter will frame them for me. Painting is a most acceptable occupation for young ladies, after all."

She trotted back to the house, Polly watching with amused affection not unmingled with dismay. Apparently two parlours and two maids were giving rise to pretensions of gentility. Mrs. Howard had never before claimed to be anything more than a respectable woman, and here she was bestowing the status of "young lady" on her daughter.

Of course it was perfectly proper, expected even, for young ladies to sketch and to paint in watercolours. Producing and selling oil paintings was another matter altogether. Polly had no aspirations to join the ranks of the gentry and she could only hope their new neighbours would not be offended by her mother's putting on airs above her station.

To call her young was equally inaccurate. Was not Mama herself forever telling her that it was time to start wearing a spinster's cap? Not that she ever remembered.

Dismissing the thought, she returned to her work. She set up her easel and propped on it the canvas on which she had sketched Kolya in charcoal, then spread her drawings of him on the table.

He laughed up at her from the paper, the slanted eyes that had first attracted her interest now less important than their expression. Was he a gentleman after all? For a wistful moment Polly wished she really were a lady. The gulf between the gentry and the middle classes seemed as wide as that between the middle class and the labourer she had thought him to be.

It was growing too dark to paint. She went into the house to change for dinner.

The next morning, dressed in an old gown, she went out to her studio right after breakfast and put on her bedaubed smock. She was determined to work on Kolya's portrait, in the unacknowledged hope that completing it would exorcise his haunting image from her mind.

She knew already that the tone of the painting was to be a warm golden brown. That was how she saw him. She closed her eyes and envisioned her first sight of him, waiting at the bottom of the Pantiles steps: crisp, light brown curls, weather-bronzed face, hazel eyes, threadbare brown jacket. Patient and humble he had appeared, until she fell into his arms and saw the amusement in his face.

And then the spilt turpentine, the greedy terrier, his timely reminder that she had lost her loaf of bread. Even then he had seemed to understand and excuse her absentmindedness.

If she had supposed for a moment that he was a gentleman, she would never have been so forward as to ask him to sit for her. But she had not known. She had sent him to buy bread, had walked home with him carrying her basket. Daydreaming, Polly wandered through her all too brief acquaintance with Kolya until she came to the last moment.

She had met him at the front door of the new house. Her mother had called her, and Ned was waiting to take him to Five Oaks.

"Good-bye," she had said hurriedly. "And good luck." It was inadequate but no other words came to mind.

"*Do svidaniya,* Miss Howard." His tone had been light and teasing, inconsequential. He had smiled down at her, then bowed and kissed her hand.

Polly sighed. She had long since decided that the kiss was a meaningless gesture, a mere Continental habit. Opening her eyes, she set about mixing the colours for the imprimatura.

"Polly!" On the gravel path, Nick sounded like a herd of elephants. The door flung open. "Polly, guess what! Kolya is here."

She stared at him.

"Kolya, the Russian," he said with exaggerated patience. "You remember him? Tall, thin, had the most amazing adventures?"

"Of course I remember him, you silly boy. He's here?"

Nick groaned. "Did I not just say so? In the drawing room with Mother. She says you're to come quick."

"Yes, of course, at once," she said in a daze. She set down her palette and brush on the table and hurried out.

Following her, Nick continued, "Ned went out, and Mother needs your help to entertain the Danvilles. You should see Lord John's curricle — slap up to the echo! — and a pair of spanking greys. D'you think Ned will teach me to drive the gig?"

Polly scarcely heard him. She sped to the drawing room. Pausing on the threshold she saw, sitting opposite the door, a young lady in a carriage dress of straw-coloured gros de Naples ornamented with bows of mahogany velvet down the front and around the hem. Her velvet bonnet matched the dress and boasted three curling, mahogany-dyed ostrich plumes. She smiled shyly at Polly.

Behind her stood a large, dark, handsome gentleman, who nodded. Polly's gaze moved on and found her mother's aghast face. Suddenly she realised that she was still wearing her painting smock.

"Lady John," Mrs. Howard said bravely, "may I present my daughter?"

"How do you do, Miss Howard?" If her ladyship was shocked by Polly's appearance, her soft voice and delicate features gave no hint of it.

Polly curtsied, smiling at her, already determined to paint her some day.

Her husband bowed. "Miss Howard." He looked more amused than offended by her disgraceful apparel. "I understand you are acquainted with my friend, Volkov."

Turning, she came face to face with Kolya. For a moment all she was aware of was his eyes laughing at her, and her heart leaped with gladness. Then she noticed that he was elegantly clad in a close-fitting tan riding coat, starched cravat tied in an immaculate Waterfall, spotless buckskin breeches, and glossy black boots. How could she ever have supposed he was anything other than a gentleman?

What a quiz he must think her, bursting into the room in her painting clothes. Her cheeks grew hot and she stammered, "P-pray excuse me. I left my brushes out. I must go and wash them."

He put out a detaining hand. "May I go

with you, Miss Howard? *Madame* tells me you have a new studio. I should like to see."

"Volkov has told us that you are an artist, Miss Howard," said Lord John. "One day we should like to see your work, should we not, my dear?" He laid a hand on his wife's shoulder. "But not today, I think, as we have a number of other calls to make. We just wanted to welcome you to Loxwood, ma'am, Miss Howard. Kolya, we shall see you later."

The Danvilles made their farewells and departed, Nick dashing out after them to see the bang-up curricle bowl away down the lane. Still feeling flustered, Polly took Kolya — Mr. Volkov, she must call him now — out to the back garden.

As they walked towards the studio, she noticed that he was walking awkwardly.

"You are limping," she exclaimed. "Have you hurt yourself?"

"No, ma'am, but I am wearing Danville's boots." He sighed ruefully. "Are the excellent boots, but his feet are shorter and wider than mine. Is easy to change the size of the clothes. The feetwear are more difficult."

"Much more difficult," she agreed, laughing. Her bashfulness fled at the realization that his finery was borrowed. She hoped Lord John was going to have some "feetwear" made to measure for his friend. "I did not expect to see you again," she confessed.

"Did I not say to you *do svidaniya?*" He was teasing.

"What does that mean?"

"Is same as French *au revoir.* Until we meet."

"Well, how could I have guessed? Here is my studio. Dear Ned had it all ready for me when we arrived."

He looked around. "Is good. I may see the pictures?"

Polly hesitated. She had a score or so of paintings that she had kept because she was particularly fond of them, or because Mr. Irving had not thought them suitable for display in his shop. To be sure, visitors to the Wells had bought her work, but that did not mean it was fit to be displayed to a cosmopolitan gentleman like Kolya — Mr. Volkov.

She knew that the Russian army had looted Paris and carried off to St Petersburg half the art treasures that Napoleon had stolen from all over Europe. As an officer in that army, Mr. Volkov had probably seen them.

"You do not want to show, I will not press," he said gently.

"No, no, you may look. I just hope you are not expecting too much."

The partitioned crates provided by the carter had proved an efficient way to store the pictures. The first one Kolya pulled out was of an apple tree in bloom. Its delicate white and pink blossoms were silhouetted against the far-off hills of the common and a pale blue sky set with puffy clouds whose sunrise glow faintly echoed the pink of the petals.

"Khorosho!" said Kolya, sounding surprised. "Is good." He balanced it on the side of the box, leaning against the wall, and stepped back to look from a distance. "Is excellent."

His surprise convinced Polly of his sincerity better than any protestations could. As he continued to pull one picture after another from the crates, she picked up her brush and palette and went back to work on the precise shade she wanted for the underpainting.

She was applying it to the canvas when he put the last picture away and asked, "What you are working on now?" With innate courtesy he did not move around the easel to look.

"I'm just beginning your portrait."

"You wish that I sit for you again? I can

come easily from Five Oaks. Danville has the bang-up horses and is not far."

"Will you? I'm sure it will be better if I can paint from life, not just from sketches."

"You are a true artist. You had the lessons?"

"Yes, at school. My teacher learned from Gainsborough and Sir Joshua Reynolds, and he taught Mr. Turner and John Constable." It was easy to talk to him while she was busy. "When he retired from teaching at the Royal Academy, he came to live in Tunbridge Wells. He knew lots of people and he used to take some of us to Chiddingstone and Penshurst Place to see the collections of art masterpieces. He died several years ago."

"Was an excellent teacher."

"He used to say that he had all the techniques of a great artist but insufficient imagination and dedication."

"I think you have enough imagination and dedication, *nyet?*"

"Dedication, certainly." She smiled at him, and then turned serious. "Sometimes I think my imagination is too good. I dream of holding a private exhibition one day, but it is never likely to be anything more than a fantasy."

"Nothing is impossible, Miss Howard. Is

necessary to have a dream. I have nothing, only good friends, but still I dream and I will work till dream comes true."

"What are you going to do?"

"First I learn to manage an estate, like your brother. In Russia, the farming is very backwards, you understand, and I am for a long time interested in the English agriculture. Danville says Mr. Howard is the excellent estate agent. He has turned Loxwood from the wilderness to productive farm. You think he is willing to teach me?"

"Ned?" Polly was taken by surprise. "Why, I expect so. You must ask him, but he will not be home till this evening, he said."

"I come tomorrow early, to ask and to sit for you. And I wish to ask favour of you, also."

"A favour?"

"I explain. Danville and Rebecca Ivanovna — Lady John, I should say — tell me I must learn to speak better the English since I will live in England. You do not say 'the' England?"

"No, just England."

"Ah, in French is *l'Angleterre* but I was sure is not same in English. So, they tell me I leave out 'a' and 'the' when should be used, but when I put in, they laugh and say, 'not there.' Is very complicated, I think. You will help me when I make the mistakes?"

" 'A mistake' or just 'mistakes.' You are right, it is complicated. I had never considered it before. I think you speak excellent English, though. I shall try to help but I scarcely ever notice anything wrong. Except when you say something like feetwear." Polly giggled.

"Is not right word?"

"*It* is not *the* right word. It should be footwear."

Kolya grinned and shook his head. "Is not — It is not logical, the English. Feet is the plural, foot is the singular, *nyet?* If I put on only footwear I must hop." He suited action to the word, then squawked as Lord John's boot pinched his toes. "*Chort vozmi!* I hope shoemaker works quickly."

"What does *chort vozmi* mean?" she enquired.

"It is not good for a young lady to say these words," Kolya reproved her, then laughed. "I see there is advantage to live in a foreign country. When I swear, the ladies will not be shocked."

"I may not have understood the words," said Polly serenely, "but I could tell very well from your tone of voice that you should not have been saying them."

That made him laugh still more. When he had recovered from his mirth sufficiently to sit still, he posed for her for an hour or so, before saying he must go as the Danvilles expected him. Soon after, Ella called her in for luncheon.

Only her mother was there, far too gratified by the Danvilles' visit of welcome to give Polly more than a perfunctory scold for appearing in her smock. Nick had taken some sandwiches and gone off exploring. Polly decided to follow suit that afternoon, looking for good places to set up her easel, but she was forestalled by the arrival of the vicar and his wife.

The Reverend and Mrs. Wyndham were duly impressed by Mrs. Howard's carefully casual mention of the Danvilles' morning call. They had already heard that a mysterious foreigner was staying at Five Oaks and Mrs. Wyndham was openly agog for further news. Their hostess was no scandalmonger. She told them only that she had met Mr. Volkov and understood that he was a Russian. Her genteel reserve did her no discredit in their eyes. When the vicar pleaded urgent business and departed, Mrs. Wyndham stayed behind to drink a dish of tea.

Pleased that her mother had so soon found a new friend, Polly submitted patiently to an afternoon of excruciating boredom.

When the vicar's wife left, Mrs. Howard went to the kitchen to check on preparations for dinner. Passing the kitchen door on her way to the studio, Polly heard her mother's wail.

"Oh Nicky, what have you been doing?"

She looked in. Mrs. Howard, Mrs. Coates, and Ella were all staring at the scullery doorway where Nick stood. He was plastered to the knees with mud, which was also liberally bedaubed elsewhere upon his person, and he wore a look of injured innocence.

"Nothing. Just fishing. I brought a couple of bream for dinner, but if you don't want 'em . . ." He stepped backwards, squelching.

"Fresh bream do make a tasty mouthful," Mrs. Coates assured him.

"Now don't you stir till you've stripped off every stitch you're wearing, Master Nick." Glaring at the cook, Ella asserted the right of a longtime family servant. "Right down to your drawers. It's a hot bath you'll be needing."

As everything appeared to be under control, Polly went on her way. Behind her she heard Nick's voice.

"I met a famous fellow, Mother. He lent me proper fishing tackle today, and tomorrow he's going to take me out shooting rabbits."

That remark did not seem calculated to soothe a mother's anxious heart. Polly hurried her steps in the opposite direction.

She worked in the studio until dusk, according Ned no more than a brief wave when he looked in after stabling Chipper. He shook his head with a grin as he strolled towards the house. He had forgotten just how single-minded she was.

For several years he had been forced to be equally single-minded. He had worked very hard but now the estate was running smoothly. Instead of spending his evenings catching up on bookkeeping and business correspondence, he had time to spare for reading and conversation. It was a joy to have his family about him.

Nick appeared at the back door. "Ned, Ma says I'm not to go out rabbit-shooting tomorrow."

It was a joy, Ned assured himself silently, to have his family about him.

Diligent enquiry revealed that his

brother's "famous fellow" was the eldest son of Sir Robert Brent, the squire of Alfold Crossways, a neighbouring village. Ned had himself taught Nick to shoot during his summer holidays last year, but it took some time to persuade his mother that her little boy was old enough to take out a gun. Ned went up to change for dinner determined to write tomorrow to the duke to request his influence in finding Nick a midshipman's berth.

Fortunately his Grace's brother was a Lord of the Admiralty, so it should not take too long.

At dinner, Ned told his family that Lord John had asked him to take Mr. Volkov about with him on his daily business and to explain to him the management of an estate. "His lordship offered to pay me for my pains," he added, helping himself to a large piece of fish. Mrs. Coates had cooked the bream with a pinch of lemon thyme, and its smell made his mouth water.

"Mr. Volkov told me he is eager to learn," Polly said. "I believe he hopes to find a post as an overseer, for he has nothing. Nothing but good friends, he said. Shall you help him, Ned?"

"Yes, but I shall not take the money. Lord John insisted that the payments should be kept secret. I daresay Mr. Volkov is too proud to accept it and I would not have him think I was doing for friendship what I was actually being paid for."

"A nice scruple." Mrs. Howard sounded doubtful.

"I think it's splendid of you," said Nick. "Pass the potatoes, please, Mother, I'm starving. I'm glad you like Kolya after all, Ned. He's a great gun. You must ask him to tell you all his adventures."

"Mr. Volkov is going to sit for me."

Polly's statement was met with silence. Nick had his mouth full of steak-and-kidney pie, and Mrs. Howard looked as dismayed as Ned felt.

After a moment, he said, "I cannot think it wise."

"Most unwise," his mother seconded him. "Indeed, Polly dear, it would not be proper."

"He did before," she pointed out, unruffled.

"But we did not know then that he was a gentleman."

"I cannot see that it makes the slightest difference. It is all arranged. He is coming tomorrow."

Ned knew it was useless to argue. Polly had the faraway look in her eyes which

84

meant she was planning a picture. She went on eating automatically, and she did not even hear Mrs. Howard's continued protests.

After dinner she took a lantern and went out to the studio. Nick asked if he could borrow Ned's fowling piece next day and went to his brother's tiny bookroom-cum-office to clean the gun. Ned and his mother settled by the fire in the sitting room.

"What are we going to do about Polly and Mr. Volkov?" Mrs. Howard asked anxiously, setting neat stitches in the wristband of the shirt she was making.

"I don't know. She positively glows when he is mentioned. What can we do? She is of age and he is an intimate friend of my employer. I cannot forbid him the house. But a match is out of the question. Though he may be a gentleman, it seems he has not a penny to his name."

"Then you think he has serious intentions? I cannot be so sanguine. After all, Polly has no money either, and she is not merely of age, she is on the shelf by anyone's calculation. No, he is looking to amuse himself. We must hope that a flirtation is all he has in mind," she added ominously.

"You mean . . . ? Surely he would not . . . she would not . . . ! She is not a chambermaid, nor a farm girl, after all. And for all Lord John was a Buck of the first stare before his marriage, I never heard that he had dealings with any but the muslin company — begging your pardon, Mother. He will warn Volkov off. No, I will not believe Polly is in danger of anything worse than a broken heart, and Lord knows that is bad enough."

6

"Good day, Ella. I come to sit for Miss Howard."

"Good day to 'e, sir, and a fine day it is. Come in, do, but it's my belief Miss Polly's still out."

"We have appointed time for eleven o'clock." Kolya sighed. "I shall tell Mr. Howard to give her a watch."

"That wouldn't do no good, sir. Miss Polly'd just forget to look at it when she's got her mind on her pitchers."

He smiled and shook his head. "Yes, you are right. You not know which way she went?"

"Kolya!" Nick bounced out of the dining room. "I mean Mr. Volkov. Have you been out with Ned, sir? Are you looking for Polly? She was down by the stream, drawing the bridge. She had me sitting on it for half an hour, pretending to fish," he added in disgust. "Shall I fetch her, or show you the way? It's just round the corner."

"Thank you, I will find."

Mrs. Howard emerged from the sitting room, looking worried as usual. "Mr. Volkov, I thought I heard your voice. Polly told me she is expecting you, but she is not yet come home, I fear. It is shockingly discourteous of her."

"I know Miss Howard means no harm, *madame,* and Master Nick has told me where to find."

She looked flustered. "Nick, go with Mr. Volkov and show him the way, and then stay with your sister."

Nick complied without the expected argument. As they strolled down the village street, Kolya asked him why he had been indoors on a sunny morning.

"Ned found some naval charts and a book about navigation in the library at the manor," he explained, grimacing. "Lord John gave him leave to borrow them for me. I'm sure they'd be very interesting on a rainy day. Still, Bob Brent has to con his book in the mornings too, so I'm to meet him at noon. I don't see that I need stay with you and Polly, do you, sir?"

Kolya knew perfectly well what was in Mrs. Howard's mind. Yesterday she had insisted on staying uncomfortably in the studio throughout his sitting. Polly had been too absorbed in her work to take much notice of her mother's sudden insistence on chaperoning her. Kolya was amused. Anyone who knew Polly's dedication to her art must be aware that dalliance was the furthest thing from her mind when she was painting.

"I expect she will want to go back to the studio," he said to Nick. "Is no need to stay, I think."

"Oh yes, that's right. Then I'll be off, sir. You see the bridge?" He pointed. "Beside it there's a path going down to the bank and she's just down there. Look, you can see her from here, with all those wretched brats about her." Nick snorted in disgust, then strode off, whistling a merry tune.

Kolya stopped in the middle of the bridge and leaned on the parapet. Polly was sitting by the slow, meandering stream, where trailing waterweed like mermaids' hair rippled the surface of the greenish water. Beside her stood a pollarded willow, a giant's spiked mace. In her sage green pelisse and faded straw hat she could have been the inhabitant of a fairy tale, a wood sprite, casting a spell on the cottage on the opposite bank. Gnomes in brown homespun clustered about her.

Kolya laughed at his fancy. Like many of the local buildings, the cottage she was sketching had a brick lower storey and an upper storey hung with rounded tiles. He thought it must be difficult to draw. At any rate, Polly was so absorbed in her work that she had not noticed his arrival, though now and then she addressed a smiling remark to her audience of wondering village children.

As he picked his way down the narrow, muddy path to her side, the children scattered.

"Kolya! I mean, Mr. Volkov." Her smile of greeting made him forget any lingering exasperation at her absentmindedness. "Is it eleven already? I forgot to listen to the church clock."

She was half guilty, half laughing. Rather than seem to reproach her, he avoided the question. "I come to escort you back to the studio."

"That is kind of you, but I have decided I want to paint you outdoors, perhaps on horseback. The light in the studio seemed too cold this morning, when outside is all golden April sunshine."

"Is not enough room here for my horse," he pointed out. He wanted to remove her from this spot where they might be seen together by any passing busybody. "Besides, better you finish first the picture you have started. Perhaps we sit in the garden?" That would be the perfect place, hidden from prying eyes yet visible from the house, so not needing a chaperone.

"Yes, I have done so little perhaps we could," she said consideringly. Already lost in thought, she gave him her sketch book and folded her little canvas stool.

He took it from her, tucked it under his arm with the sketch book, and helped her up the muddy slope to the road. She was hardly aware of his presence, his hand under her elbow. He was reminded of walking with her to her home in Tunbridge Wells — but then he had been a ragged fellow. Now he was once more clad as befitted his station, though not in the magnificent green and red uniform of the tsar's own *Preobrazhensky* regiment of the Imperial Guard. Colonel Prince Nikolai Mikhailovich Volkov, eldest son of the Minister, was not accustomed to being ignored by young ladies, even of the highest rank.

Though he laughed at himself, he was piqued.

Polly drifted at his side, not speaking until they turned into the drive which led to the back of the house, their feet crunching on gravel.

"Yes," she said then with satisfaction, "I believe I can transfer it outside without much change, which probably means I ought never to have tried it indoors in the first place. Will you sit on the bench under the cherry tree?"

For the next hour Kolya had no cause to complain of neglect. When her gaze was not on his face it was on his growing likeness on the canvas. She asked him to tell her about Russia, and he knew she was listening because her questions were intelligent and to the point. Having once completed the planning in her head and taken up pencil or brush, she worked by a sort of instinct combined with practised technique which required only part of her attention.

The only thing she was completely unconscious of was the passage of time.

"Miss Polly," Ella called from the back door, "the master's home and the missus wants to know if you mean to eat your luncheon. And she says to ask Mr. Volkov if he'll kindly step in and take a bite."

"Already? All right, Ella, we are coming. Will you be able to stay a little longer after luncheon, sir?"

He was tempted. He had always been an active man, but after the ceaseless struggle for survival of the past few months it was pleasant to lounge in the sun and talk to a pretty girl.

There was a soothing quality to Polly's listening. Kolya realised that in describing his country, as opposed to the adventure stories he had told Nick, he was somehow letting go of it, setting himself outside it. In spite of his determination to build a new life in England, he had been unknowingly clinging to the idea of going home. Holy Mother Russia must be put behind him. Tsar Aleksandr would never forgive an officer who had flouted his authority, and Tsar Aleksandr was in his prime. It might be thirty years before a new reign brought the hope of pardon.

They had reached the house before he said, "I am sorry, Miss Howard, but your brother is expecting that I go with him again this afternoon. I must learn. I do not mean forever to sponge on my friends." Enough of solemnity. He grinned. "Is fine English idiom, *nyet?*"

She laughed and nodded, pleased with his pleasure.

The April days slipped past, sunshine sparkling after showers, green buds bursting on oak and elm, the cherry in bloom and every coppice carpeted with bluebells reflecting the sky. In St Petersburg the ice on the Neva would be breaking up with its thunderous, crackling roar, but Kolya had no time to think of St Petersburg.

He found his studies unexpectedly fascinating, and his admiration for Ned Howard's expertise grew. As they rode about the estate, overseeing drainage and ploughing and planting, dealing with tenants' problems, he told Ned what be knew of farming in Russia.

Serfs with nothing to gain from their labours were lazy and careless, and they strongly resisted any attempt to introduce modern methods. Kolya did not tell Ned that once he had planned to free his serfs as soon as he inherited the vast Volkov estates. That moment would never come. To reveal that his father was Prince Volkov, one of the wealthiest and most influential men in Russia, was worse than pointless: it might spoil his friendship with the Howards.

Even thinking him merely a private gentleman, Ned was always deferential to his pupil, though he would have scorned to toad-eat. Polly, on the other hand, had not a deferential bone in her body. She treated with the same placid friendliness the village children who gathered around her easel and Rebecca Ivanovna, Lady John Danville, whom Kolya brought one afternoon to see her paintings.

When her ladyship bought a flower study and agreed to sit for her portrait after removing to Loxwood Manor, Polly was pleased, but she did not fawn.

Kolya flattered himself that for him Polly's smile was just a bit brighter than for anyone else, her greeting more eager, her leave-taking tinged with regret. That did not mean that she learned punctuality to please him. Often when he arrived for his sittings, he had to chase off after her across the countryside. She would be sitting on a knoll, under an oak tree, sketching Five Oaks; or, closer to home, painting a cottage garden gay with orange pot-marigolds and heavy-scented purple stocks, or the mallards in the stream with their glossy spring plumage. They would walk together back to the house, loaded with easel, box of paints, stool, huge green umbrella, and the wet canvas in its protective sling, discussing painting techniques and the philosophy of art.

She usually remembered to tell someone where she was going, but Kolya was learning the way her mind worked and soon found he could guess where she might be.

She would not let him see his own portrait. "The subject of a portrait is rarely completely satisfied," she explained with the seriousness which enchanted him, "so until I am satisfied there will always be a temptation to change it to suit the model, not myself."

The April days slipped by, and every day Kolya found himself more attracted to the absentminded artist.

In the middle of April, Lord John's cousin Lady Graylin and her husband, Sir Andrew, came to stay at Five Oaks on their way to the Continent. Sir Andrew had been posted to Switzerland as Consul General and he had promised to take Teresa to Paris *en route*, though her pregnancy was beginning to show. Lady Graylin had never allowed such minor considerations to hinder her.

Kolya had known the Graylins and their little girl in St Petersburg, and he was glad to renew the acquaintance. He also knew, from his visit to London in 1814, two of John's friends who turned up a day or two later.

"Repairing lease, don't you know," said Mr. Bevan jauntily over the port after dinner on the day of their arrival. "The Season's more exhausting than ever, what with the coronation coming up. Besides, you can't go on honeymooning for ever, old chap. Mind you, I'm not saying I blame you. Dashed restful female, Lady John, not for ever dashing about and chattering."

"She don't lie about languishing on a sofa, neither," put in Lord Fitzsimmons, who had recently inherited a barony and was forced to contemplate settling down. "Be damned if it don't make a fellow think it wouldn't be so bad to be leg-shackled after all."

"I say, no need to go so far as that, Fitz."

The rest of the gentlemen laughed at Bev's alarm, but it set Kolya to thinking. He had once seriously considered marrying Rebecca Ivanovna. Polly had the same restful quality as the younger woman, without the shyness. Of course, her dedication to art, while admirable, was bound to prove inconvenient at times, but . . . He pulled himself up — for the forseeable future he was in no position to support a wife.

"Shall we rejoin the ladies?" John suggested hopefully.

In the drawing room they found that, emboldened by Teresa's encouraging presence, Rebecca Ivanovna had decided to hold her first dinner party. She was not yet ready to tackle the local landowners, but the vicar and his wife and daughter were agreeable and uncritical, and there was a widowed Danville cousin who lived in a cottage on the estate.

"And I thought perhaps the Howards," she went on, "if you do not object, John? Mrs. Howard is a thoroughly respectable woman, and I found Miss Howard most amiable. We could send the carriage for them."

Though Kolya noticed Bev and Fitz exchanging a martyred look and a murmured "devilish flat company," John unsurprisingly gave his fond approval. Kolya offered to deliver an invitation to the Howards on the morrow.

The invitation was received by Mrs. Howard with complacency, by Ned with misgiving, and by Polly with pleasure.

"I should like to know Lady John better," she said when they discussed it at dinner that evening.

"You cannot expect to be on intimate terms with her ladyship," Ned pointed out. "Don't forget that her husband is a duke's son, and way above our touch."

"Nonsense," said Mrs. Howard. "Polly is the daughter of an officer and a gentleman, and I understand that Lady John was once a governess. It is not as if Lord John will ever be duke. Mrs. Wyndham says that his elder brother has two sons. Still," she added, "it will not do to appear encroaching."

"I don't see why I can't go," Nick grumbled. "Mr. Volkov says Lord Fitzsimmons and Mr. Bevan are top-o'-the-trees Corinthians. I want to meet them. Are you sure the invitation was not for me too, Mother?"

"No, dear, of course not."

"But I . . ."

"Pray do not be forever arguing, Nicholas. Polly, is your blue silk fit to wear? Oh dear, it must be new trimmed at least, I'm sure, and the village shop has nothing fit for it. What are we going to do?"

Ned came to the rescue. "Don't worry, Mother, I can drive you into Billingshurst tomorrow afternoon."

"Thank you, dear. Miss Pettinger told me that Billingshurst has a very adequate haberdasher, and Mrs. Bruton patronises an excellent seamstress there if ever we have need of new evening gowns."

"Why, Mother, I'm always quite content with gowns of your making. Ned, shall you leave Mr. Volkov on his own tomorrow? Is he a good pupil?"

"He's enthusiastic and learns very quickly, and he has a natural air of authority. He is quite capable of supervising the men for an afternoon. Everyone likes him in spite of his being a foreigner — in fact, he is very popular with the tenants already. He never forgets their names and he's always ready to pick up a fallen child or carry a heavy basket for an old woman."

"Then you think he will be a good bailiff?"

"One day, certainly. He's making an excellent start. It's knowing what crops to plant in which fields, where drainage is needed, when to send cattle to market, and so on that takes years of experience."

Polly sighed, she was not sure why. She wondered whether Kolya realised how long it would be before he was ready to run an estate on his own.

7

Polly let her mother choose the new trimming for her evening gown. Mrs. Howard had an eye for colour and style which could have done justice to a far larger budget for clothes than she was ever likely to see. The elaborate ruffles and rouleaux that were coming into fashion suited her very well, but her daughter's taller, fuller figure required simplicity.

The midnight blue silk looked most elegant with ivory lace stitched around sleeve and bodice and in deep, narrow, reversed V's rising from the hem almost to the high waist. No one could possibly guess that Honiton lace, and not the finest Brussels, adorned the gown. The only trouble was, Polly was not there to put it on.

Mrs. Howard's grey satin gown rustled agitatedly as she pattered once more to the window to peer into the lane. She even opened the casement and leaned out, conduct she would normally have stigmatized as shockingly vulgar.

"Ned, where can she be?" she wailed. "Surely Nick must have found her by now."

"I really think I had better go and search, too," he said patiently, not for the first time.

"No, you are already dressed, and very fine you look." She spared an admiring glance for his black swallow-tailed coat and pantaloons, modestly striped russet brown waistcoat and well-starched, neatly tied neckcloth with the captain's carnelian pin. "Much good it will do if Polly does not come soon. We cannot go without her."

"Perhaps we should."

"Even if she arrives this minute, we shall be shockingly late. I do not know which is most ill-bred, to arrive late, to go without her, or not to go at all."

"You had best go on your own, Mother, so as not to upset Lady John's numbers." Ned's attempt at humour fell flat.

"We shall never be invited again."

"Mother!" Nick's halloo rang through the quiet evening, followed by the sound of the church clock striking six.

"At last!" Mrs. Howard leaned out of the window again, then sank back onto the nearest chair. "Alone!" She buried her face in a handkerchief.

Nick pounded up to the window. "Can't find her anywhere. And here's the carriage," he added as the duke's barouche turned the corner. "I'll have to go instead."

His mother did not appear to find any consolation in the notion, for she burst into tears. Nick was speaking to the coachman and failed to notice this evidence of maternal affection. He returned to the window, grinning.

"Message from Mr. Volkov. He says to try the mill."

"Polly did mention the reflection of the setting sun in the mill pond," Ned said, going over to him. "You might as well try. And ask the coachman if he minds waiting."

"Right, I'm off, but . . ." He stopped as the drawing room door opened. Ned swung round.

"I'm on time for once," said Polly, looking pleased with herself.

"On time!" screeched her mother, dropping her handkerchief and surging to her feet.

"Yes. You said six o'clock and the church clock just struck six."

"Six o'clock the carriage was to pick us up. It is past six, and look at you."

Polly looked down at her serviceable brown walking dress and muddy half-boots. "Oh," she said blankly. "I forgot I have to change my gown." She raised a hand to tuck in a bothersome wisp of hair.

"Don't touch your face! You have paint on your fingers. Upstairs with you at once." She shooed her daughter out, calling, "Ella, hot water to Miss Polly's room, quickly."

Nick returned to the window from another consultation with the coachman. "He says he was told he might have to wait." He laughed. "It looks to me as if Mr. Volkov has everything well in hand."

Above-stairs, with Ella and Mrs. Howard getting in each other's way, Polly split a seam in her hurry to take off her dress. She washed, scrubbing most of the Venetian red off her hands. The church clock chimed the quarter. Her mother pulled the blue silk over her head and started doing up the tiny buttons down the back as Ella eased her feet into the blue kid slippers. She sat down at the dressing table and Ella unpinned her hair, brushed it, and replaited it.

"No time for a fancy coyffer," she mumbled through the hairpins in her mouth, fastening the braids into the usual coronet. "Too late for ringlets."

"So ill-mannered to be so late," Mrs. Howard moaned. "What will her ladyship think!"

Polly stared at herself in the mirror. Her dark eyes were wide with apprehension.

They were going to be late. Lord and Lady John would be offended. But what really mattered was that Kolya would be vexed with her for offending his friends.

Mama fastened around her neck the gold locket with Papa's dark hair curled inside. Ella draped about her shoulders her cloak of blue *velours simulé,* put her bonnet on her head and tied it, and handed her her gloves. Pulling them on, she followed her mother down the stairs as the clock chimed the half.

Late, late, late, late, sang the bells. Late, late, late, late.

"Don't look so down-pin," Ned whispered as he handed her into the barouche. "You did your best."

She squeezed his hand, grateful but uncomforted.

The horses trotted along the winding lanes with agonizing slowness. Polly imagined messages being sent to the kitchen, the cook getting hotter and crosser, the fowls on the spit drying out and blackening. Only a sunset which swirled across the sky in swathes of rose and lemon distracted her, and it was over all too soon.

At last the carriage turned into the long avenue leading up to Five Oaks. Polly had only seen the Palladian mansion from a distance, impressive and beautiful but merely part of a wide landscape. As they approached, the vast building loomed in the twilight, its pillared façade stretching endlessly ahead. And its inhabitants were all being kept waiting by Polly's tardiness. She cringed.

The entrance hall was a marble cavern. The stately butler met the Howards with no hint of disapproval, but then his face might also have been carved in marble for all the expression it showed. An equally impassive footman in green livery trimmed with red was divesting Polly of her cloak, when Kolya strode into the hall.

He was grinning. Even, Polly thought indignantly, on the edge of laughter. Bowing, he welcomed them to Five Oaks.

"What is so funny?" she hissed as her mother, looking distinctly nervous, and Ned followed the butler across the echoing chamber.

He offered his arm and urged her after the others. "You are early, Miss Howard. This I did not expect."

"Early!"

"Not too early," he quickly soothed her ruffled feelings. "One guest is not here yet. But I thought I had planned all so that you will come at precisely twenty to eight o'clock, and it is only half past the seven."

"You planned it?" She was puzzled.

"I arranged that the coach came at six o'clock, with the message for young Nick to find you by the mill pond in plenty time. You were not by the mill?"

"Yes, I was. But I remembered to listen for the church clock and I was home by six."

It was Kolya's turn to be puzzled. "Then why you are not here even earlier?"

"I forgot I needed time to change my dress."

He burst into laughter. "This I forgot also!" He stopped and turned her to face him. "I did not look before — was looking at your face only. Is most elegant gown, with the beautiful woman inside." His slanting eyes were serious now.

Polly felt hot all over, hot enough to melt inside. Fortunately, at that moment the butler opened a door and announced the Howards, and she and Kolya hurried to catch up. In the swarm of introductions which followed she forgot her embarrassment — and the peculiar sensation which had accompanied it.

Far from overwhelming with splendour, the drawing room was a comfortable apartment, though several superb pictures hung on the walls. Polly recognized a Canaletto, and she thought one of the portraits might be a Van Dyck. She tore her eyes away and concentrated on the introductions.

She had scarcely taken a seat when the gentleman who had been presented as Lord Fitzsimmons materialized at her side. Of middling height and slight build, he had classically perfect features and golden locks which might have been envied by Apollo. Though his bottle green coat and brown pantaloons were elegantly restrained, a green satin waistcoat embroidered with daisies, a profusion of fobs, and an intricately tied cravat hinted at a sternly repressed tendency to dandyism. His bright blue eyes held an expression of ingenuous enthusiasm.

"May I join you, ma'am?" Receiving permission, he sat down at her side. "Understand you paint. M'sister Julia was a dab at watercolours before she married. Expect she would have had a go at the river here. I daresay you have painted it?"

It soon became apparent that what he really wanted to talk about was the splendid fishing to be found in the River Arun, which ran through the Five Oaks park. Polly reciprocated with stories of Nick's angling prowess, which all the family had heard so often they could have repeated them word for word. She also told him that she had seen several large fish in the Loxwood mill pond, jumping for flies at dusk.

"I say, ma'am, good of you to mention it," he said, and as he took her in to dinner she heard him mutter approvingly to Mr. Bevan as he passed, "Sensible female!"

To her disappointment, she was not seated next to Kolya at the dinner table. He sat opposite, but remembering her mother's instructions Polly made no attempt to converse with him. Though she had never before attended a formal dinner party, she was not at all apprehensive of making mistakes. It seemed unlikely that she would do anything truly dreadful, and everyone was surely too amiable not to forgive any minor errors of etiquette.

The elderly vicar of Billingshurst, on her right, was a gentle, vague man who probably would not have noticed if she had eaten her fish with a soup spoon. On her other side, Lord Fitzsimmons was flatteringly eager to converse, and to pile her plate with interesting and irresistible delicacies. Polly enjoyed both her dinner and his inconsequential chatter.

She caught Kolya's eye across the table and smiled at him. He winked. He was having a difficult time with the vicar's daughter, a spinster of uncertain years who seemed to speak in homilies. Polly was glad to see him laughing with his other neighbour, Lady Graylin, a dark, striking woman whom she would have liked to paint. The Graylins, however, were leaving for Paris on the morrow. Along with Polly's disappointment at losing a prospective model, she felt an odd, inexplicable sense of relief.

When Lady John led the female exodus from the dining room, leaving the gentlemen to port and brandy, Polly found herself beside her hostess.

"As I mentioned the other day, Miss Howard, I do not know much about paintings," said her ladyship apologetically as they entered the drawing room. "However, I understand his Grace has an excellent collection. I hope you will feel free to come and inspect them one day soon. We shall be here for another fortnight or so before we remove to Loxwood Manor."

"Thank you, my lady, I should love to. You do not mind if I take a closer look now at those in this room?"

"Not at all. Let me hold a light for you." Lady John took up a branch of candles and they went to stand in front of the Canaletto.

The Grand Canal of Venice stretched before them, busy with gondolas and schooners, lined with palaces and churches stretching into the distance.

"It reminds me a little of St Petersburg," Lady John said, and she shivered as if struck by a sudden chill. "There are canals lined with palaces there, too. I was imprisoned in a fortress on one of the islands, you know," she went on doggedly, her soft voice shaking. "Nikolai Mikhailovich rescued me — that is why he was exiled."

"Kolya? Mr. Volkov?" Polly asked, astonished. "No wonder you were both happy to see him."

"He did it for the sake of his friendship with John, though he was fond of me also, I believe. Miss Howard, you will think me monstrous interfering, but I must tell you what John told me then. He said that Nikolai Mikhailovich is a rake."

"You mean he has designs upon my virtue?"

Her ladyship looked shocked at such bluntness. "Good gracious, no. I'm sure John exaggerated, but it's true, I fear, that Kolya is a shocking flirt."

Polly was almost disappointed. Of course her principles would never allow her to give in to the seductive wiles of a rake. All the same, there was something attractive in the idea of a life divided between her work and Kolya, and if he were not her husband, he would not be able to make her stop painting.

Misinterpreting her silence, Lady John said sadly, "Now you will tell me that it is none of my business and never speak to me again."

"Of course I will not. I know that your words are kindly meant. But indeed, Mr. Volkov does not flirt with me, my lady. Or hardly ever," she added, trying to be honest. "Most of all he is an interesting model, though we talk of a hundred subjects while I paint and I hope I can say he is my friend."

"And you are not offended?"

"Indeed I am not." Polly touched her hand in reassurance. The subject was dropped and they moved on to another picture.

Despite her dismissal of Lady John's warning, Polly was left vaguely uneasy. When the gentlemen joined the ladies, she was quite glad that Kolya stood talking to Ned for long enough to allow Mr. Bevan to take the seat beside her. Not that she had the least expectation that Mr. Volkov meant to rush to her side. She gave Mr. Bevan her attention. Lord John's friend was plainly a Corinthian. Though not tall he was well muscled, and his coat was cut with an eye to comfort rather than elegance. His face was engagingly ugly, with a lantern jaw and slightly crooked nose, doubtless the result of an unfortunate encounter at Gentleman Jackson's Boxing Saloon.

Unwittingly, Mr. Bevan set Polly's mind at rest with his first words. "At last I have you all to myself, Miss Howard," he declaimed dramatically. "I have been ready to call Fitz out for monopolizing you since you glided through the door like Mozart's Queen of the Night and cast your magic spell on my heart."

Now that, thought Polly, was flirting. Kolya had never made the slightest attempt to pay her such an extravagant compliment.

"Surely the Queen of the Night should have black hair, sir?" she suggested.

"Never!" He cast a half-laughing, half-apologetic glance at Lady Graylin, seated nearby, whose hair was glossy black, then turned back to Polly. "Yours shines like the harvest moon."

Lord Fitzsimmons leaned over the back of the sofa and murmured discreetly in his friend's ear, "Sorry, my boy, but the Queen of the Night's a bad lot."

Mr. Bevan was unabashed. "I tend to sleep through operas," he told Polly with aplomb. "Ought to stick to mythology and poetry. 'Queen and goddess, chaste and fair . . . ,' that's the ticket."

"Huntress," Fitz advised him. " 'Queen and huntress.' "

"Dash it, Fitz, does Miss Howard look like one of those ghastly females who chase about the hunting field covered in mud and ruin the sport? Don't hunt, do you, Miss Howard?" he added as an anxious after-thought.

"No, I confess to being on the fox's side. They are beautiful animals."

"There you are," said Bev triumphantly. " 'Queen and goddess, fair and kind.' That's how it ought to be written."

To her amusement he continued to spout flattering nonsense until the tea tray was brought in. Shortly thereafter Ned announced that they must be on their way. Polly was surprised when both Mr. Bevan and Lord Fitzsimmons begged her permission to call, but as she liked them both she readily granted it.

It was Kolya, however, who put her cloak around her shoulders. "You have enjoyed self?" he asked, smiling down at her with his hands resting lightly on her shoulders.

"Very much."

"It will be late when you come to home tonight. Tomorrow morning you will sleep late."

"I shall be up long before eleven."

"So I come at usual time?"

"At the usual time." She nodded. "I shall finish your portrait in a day or two, if it does not rain."

Mrs. Howard broke in. "Polly, the carriage is waiting."

"Until tomorrow then, Miss Howard."

As the carriage rolled homeward, Polly admitted to herself that Kolya's portrait could have been finished long since, in spite of the occasional interruption of a rainy day, if she had concentrated instead of talking to him.

8

Kolya arrived late at the Howards' on the morning after the dinner party. He and Ned had been at the far end of the Loxwood estate, talking to the gamekeeper at his cottage in the woods. The English custom of taking pains to protect the pheasants, even providing special breeding grounds, just so as to be able to go out and shoot them later, amused Kolya. In Russia, wild game was wild, and one did not shoot domestic fowl.

When he reached the gate from the meadow into the Howards' garden, he saw that Polly had already set up her easel in the usual place. She was sitting on the bench where he always posed, on a white carpet of cherry blossom petals, but she was not precisely waiting for him.

Beside her sat Mr. Bevan, and Lord Fitzsimmons lounged against the nearest tree. She was laughing.

Kolya turned his horse loose to graze. Leaning with folded arms on the top of the gate, he thoughtfully regarded the merry group. He had delighted to watch Polly enjoying herself in company last night, but somehow he was less content to see her in such high spirits today. This was his time, the time he looked forward to every morning and recalled with pleasure every evening.

He shrugged his shoulders and opened the gate. The portrait was nearly done. One morning's delay would give him more time to invent a good reason for continuing to visit Polly regularly once the painting was finished. No doubt the gentlemen would soon be on their way back to London and the delights of the Season.

As he approached, unnoticed, he saw that Mr. Bevan wore a frown of intense concentration.

"I'll give my oath there's a bit of verse with Polly in it," he was saying. "Dashed if I can recall it though."

Lord Fitzsimmons and Polly exchanged a glance and launched into a ragged chorus in two different keys.

"Polly, put the kettle on; Polly, put the kettle on . . ."

"No, no, can't be the one I was thinking of," protested the discomfitted Corinthian.

"Indeed, sir, I know how to boil a kettle," Polly assured him, laughing again, "and even how to make tea, though my cooking leaves somewhat to be desired."

"Volkov!" Lord Fitzsimmons had spotted him. "Dashed fine picture Miss Howard's painted. Caught you to the life."

"Thank you, my lord," Polly said, but Kolya decided she looked sceptical of his lordship's credentials as an art critic. She stood up and went to contemplate the canvas on the easel.

"M'sister never could get noses quite right," Fitz went on. "Always seemed to come out looking like Bev's beak."

"I say, don't insult my phiz or I'll rearrange yours to match," said Mr. Bevan with mock bellicosity. "Tell you what, ma'am, I'll commission a portrait from you if you promise to straighten my nose."

"Oh no, I could not do that," Polly said absently. "It gives your face character."

"Yes, but what sort of character?" enquired Fitz, grinning. "Positively villainous, wouldn't you say, ma'am?"

Not for the first time, Kolya wondered at the English sense of humour. If a Russian gentleman had issued such insults, he would have found himself facing pistols at dawn. In their peculiar way, the English were much saner.

He stopped beside Polly. Now that Bev

and Fitz had seen his portrait, it was difficult to obey her oft-repeated injunction not to look. Instead, he watched her face as she studied it with the faraway gaze he knew so well.

"The hands," she said. "Today I want to work on the hands." She looked up at him, a smile on her delectable lips.

"You are occupied today. You will not want to paint."

"But I do. Pray take your place while I fetch my smock."

"A long-standing engagement, gentlemen," Kolya explained smugly as she headed for the studio.

"You mean we are dismissed?" Bev sighed. "Alas that beauty should prove so cruel."

Polly returned, quite unconscious of the effect on the gentlemen of her appearance in her voluminous, multicoloured painting smock. Kolya watched in amusement as their startled expressions were speedily brought under control.

"We'll be off, Miss Howard," Lord Fitzsimmons said. "Will you be painting the mill pond this evening? You will not object if I bring my fishing rod to try for some of those brutes you spotted?"

"An angler will make a good addition to

my picture, my lord."

Not to be outdone, Bev asked if she would care to go out for a spin in his curricle on the morrow.

"That will be delightful, sir. I don't suppose you could drive me into Horsham?"

"Anywhere, Miss Howard," said Mr. Bevan expansively. "Anywhere at all."

Kolya hid a smile. Polly would make use of both her new admirers in the interests of her art: Lord Fitzsimmons as the figure of a fisherman, a rôle Nick had no patience for; and Mr. Bevan to convey her local landscapes to the bookseller in Horsham to be sold, an errand Ned had no time for.

The gentlemen were turning to leave and Polly was picking up her palette and brush when Kolya saw a strange figure, tall but hunched, struggling with the catch of the meadow gate he had just come through.

"Kakovo chorta!" he exclaimed. "Is Nicholas!" He jumped to his feet and hurried to help.

The others swung round as Nick succeeded in opening the gate one-handed. He was wet, muddy, and in his shirtsleeves, and on his shoulders he carried a small child with tangled blonde curls, wrapped in his coat.

"Nick, what happened?" asked Polly,

joining them. "Who is she?"

"Dashed if I know," said her brother, lifting the little girl down. Lost in the folds of the jacket, she clung to his leg, hiding her face. "I was with Bob Brent walking across the fields and we saw her playing by a stream. There were some ducks with babies. I think she must have tried to reach them. Anyway, she fell in and I fished her out. There was no one else around and no farms or cottages nearby, and she couldn't tell me where she came from, so I reckoned I'd best bring her home. Bob cut and run," he added in disgust.

"You were on Loxbury land?" Kolya enquired. "I know most of the tenants."

Polly knelt on the ground beside the child, who peeked at her shyly. Her face was pinched with cold. "Poor mite. She needs dry clothes and a hot drink. What is your name, pet?"

She put a dirty thumb in her mouth and glanced up at Nick.

"Tell the lady your name," he urged.

"Thuthie," she mumbled round the thumb.

"Susie?"

She nodded. Polly looked up at Kolya.

Ned had introduced him to every family on the estate. He was not sure of the names of all the children but the blonde curls were familiar. "I think I know. Is your father's name Stebbins, *golubushka?*"

Susie stared at him, her face blank.

"What's your daddy called?" Nick interpreted.

She reached up and tugged on his sleeve. He bent down and she whispered in his ear.

He broke into a grin. "Thilath Thtebbinth," he reported. "Looks like you're right, sir."

"Silas Stebbins? I know where she lives then," Kolya confirmed.

"How are we to take her home?" Rising from her knees with Kolya's assistance, Polly noticed Mr. Bevan and Lord Fitzsimmons, who were watching the proceedings from a safe distance. "Oh, I forgot. Mr. Bevan has his curricle here."

Bev looked aghast at the thought of being seen with a tousled urchin sharing his elegant equipage. "I say, Miss Howard . . ."

"I'll do it, ma'am," Lord Fitzsimmons interrupted with the air of a man nerving himself to face a horrid fate. "You won't mind if I borrow the curricle, Bev?"

Amused, Kolya glanced at Polly, but she was holding out her hand to Susie. "I must go to show the way," he pointed out. "If you will entrust the horses to me, will be no need for anyone else to go."

"Of course Bev will trust you with his horses, Volkov," his lordship said heartily and hopefully, with a look of appeal at his friend. "Danville was telling us just the other day how you taught him to drive a troika."

"Mr. Volkov is a famous whip," Nick assured Mr. Bevan. "He has won any number of races."

Bev did not appear to think this much of a recommendation but he consented gracefully.

"Susie must have dry clothes first," Polly said, "but she will not come with me. You will have to bring her, Nick. Fortunately Mama is out visiting." She shepherded her brother and the child into the house, abandoning her admirers without a backward glance.

Somewhat disgruntled, Bev took Kolya round the house to his curricle, issuing anxious instructions about his bays' tender mouths and skittish ways.

"They're a high-bred pair," Fitz agreed.

"I think I can manage them," Kolya said gravely.

Polly and Nick did not keep them waiting long. The little girl was swathed in a blue woollen shawl with a white garment under it that looked suspiciously like a pillow bere with holes cut for head and arms. Her curls were neatly combed. She still clung to Nick, who was still in his damp and dirty shirt and breeches.

"Susie starts crying if I leave her," he explained.

"I was going to go with you, to hold her," Polly said, "but I believe Nick will have to go."

"I meant to anyway. I found her, so I ought to make sure she gets home safely."

"You are a dear, Nick." Polly kissed his cheek.

Kolya saw both Mr. Bevan and Lord Fitzsimmons brighten as they realised that she would be staying with them.

He had not the slightest difficulty in driving Mr. Bevan's bays. Once he was sure of that, he turned his attention to his companion, whose face was gloomy above the child he held in his lap.

"What is wrong, Nick?"

"Bob Brent called me a milksop."

"I do not know this word."

"It means a fellow who acts like a girl."

"Because you take care of Susie?"

"Yes. But what else could I do, sir? She might have fallen in again and drowned, or wandered on and never found her way home."

"You feel bad because the friend called you milksop. Tell me how you will feel tomorrow if you hear that *devochka* is drowned?"

"Terrible." Nick shuddered. "Much worse than for any name Bob could think up. I'm glad I didn't leave her there alone."

"So, is a good feeling, *nyet?*"

"Yes, and I'll be blowed if I care what Bob Brent thinks. Besides, I can't wait till I see his face when he hears you drove me in Mr. Bevan's curricle!"

Kolya laughed. "One day I will drive you in Lord John's curricle," he promised, "and I will *spring 'em.*"

Nick was further convinced of the rightness of his action when the overjoyed Mrs. Stebbins insisted on presenting him with a freshly baked apple cake and a large cheese. Neither remained intact for more than a few minutes. Anyone would suppose that Nick was starved at home, mused Kolya, refusing a chunk of cheese hacked off with a pocketknife of doubtful cleanliness.

When they reached Loxwood it was too late for Kolya to sit for Polly as Ned was expecting him, but the portrait was finished the next day. Kolya did not have to think up an excuse to continue visiting, as Polly at once announced that she wanted to paint another. However, as the days went by, somehow the moment never arrived to begin it. She was walking with Lord Fitzsimmons or driving with Mr. Bevan, who had unwittingly stolen a march on his friend when he offered to drive him down to Five Oaks in his curricle, thus depriving him of his own vehicle.

Kolya was forced to recognize that he was jealous. There could be only one reason for jealousy — he loved Polly and wanted to marry her. He wanted to take care of her, to advance her career, but he could not even support her.

Two well-to-do Englishmen of impeccable birth were courting her. Kolya found what consolation he could in the fact that Polly apparently did not wish to paint either his lordship's perfect features or Bev's interestingly ugly mug.

One wet day at the beginning of May, Kolya arrived back at Five Oaks in the evening to find a letter waiting for him. It was franked by the Duke of Stafford. At once his hopes were aroused. Though he enjoyed learning to manage an estate, it would be years before he was competent to support himself thus. Perhaps the duke had found him a position which would allow him a modest independence at once while building towards future affluence.

Eager as he was to discover what his Grace had to say, his clothes were damp and it was time to change for dinner. He took the letter up to his chamber. A footman brought hot water and divested him of coat and boots.

Moments later, still in his shirtsleeves, Kolya was knocking at the door of John's dressing room. His lordship's valet, Pierce, admitted him.

His lordship, engaged in the serious matter of arranging his neckcloth, looked round. "Kolya, what's to do?"

"I have a letter from the duke. He has told your king how I helped you in St Petersburg. Here, read." He gave his friend the letter.

"Sit down, old chap." John was perusing the single sheet when there was a knock at the door leading to his bedchamber.

Rebecca Ivanovna peeked in. "John, are you ready to go down? Oh, I beg your pardon, I did not see that Nikolai Mikhailovich is with you."

"Come in, Beckie, love. You won't mind if she hears your news, will you, Kolya?"

"Of course not."

"What news? Good, I hope." She perched

on a stool close to her husband.

"Prinny wants to see Kolya in Brighton. He's down there sulking until he finds out whether Parliament will insist on allowing the queen to be crowned at his side, I collect. Splendid news."

"Is splendid?" Kolya was far from sure.

"If Prinny takes a liking to you, he might give you a post in his household. After all, you were aide to the emperor, so you're well qualified. At the very least, between his interest and my father's influence you are bound to find something."

"But if you do not, you will *always* be welcome at Loxwood, will he not, John?"

"Of course, always." John took her hand.

Kolya knew that they meant what they said. He knew also that John still unconsciously regarded him as a rival. There was a way to relieve him of that misapprehension.

"When the king commands, I must obey," he said with a sigh, "but I shall be sorry to go. Will be difficult to leave Miss Howard."

John looked blank.

His wife clapped her hands. "Oh, you are in love with her! I have been wondering. I'm so glad, she is charming."

"Yes, I love her. I wish to marry her." Kolya saw that John was embarrassed by his confession. An English gentleman does not reveal his emotions. Turning away, he leaned his elbows on the chest of drawers and bowed his head in his hands, for having begun he could not stem the flood of words. "I love her, but for me is no hope. I cannot support wife. She will wed Lord Fitzsimmons, whose sister stopped the painting when she married, and who will expect my Polly to stop. Or Mr. Bevan, amusing idiot who understands nothing. Perhaps is better that I leave, before I see this. I will go. Tomorrow I will go to Brighton." He raised his head.

Beckie gazed at him with sorrowful sympathy in her brown eyes.

John stood up and patted him awkwardly on the shoulder. "Frightfully sorry, old chap. I didn't realize things had come to such a pass. You shall have the carriage, of course. His Grace has a house on the Steyne where you are welcome to stay, but I daresay they will put you up at the Pavilion."

Kolya summoned up a smile. "Ah yes, Pavilion that is known as the Little Kremlin. It will be interesting to see."

"That's the spirit. Do you want me to explain your departure to Ned Howard for you?"

"No, I must thank him for his help. And will be rude, I think, not to say good-bye to Mrs. Howard, who has often given the hospitality. I shall see Polly one more time."

As he went back to his room to dress, Kolya wished he could ask Polly to wait for him, until he was able to support her. It would not be fair, since she had two eminently eligible suitors at hand.

9

Polly dashed through the drizzle to the studio. Another dank, grey day, and no doubt Fitz and Bev would be underfoot the half of it. It was all very well driving about the countryside with Mr. Bevan, discovering new scenes worthy of her brush, or chatting with Lord Fitzsimmons as she painted the picturesque pond or stream he was fishing in. Having to entertain them in the drawing room was another matter.

They kept her from her work.

Mama would not let her avoid their presence. Mama was certain that one or both gentlemen were about to come up to scratch. She had been seen casting significant looks at her daughter's suitors while whispering to the vicar's wife, who wore an air of mingled complicity and congratulation.

She might even be right about his lordship, Polly thought as she pulled on her smock. Fitz was growing more and more particular in his attentions, and kept casting out remarks about his family and his home. He was more serious-minded than Bev, whose extravagant compliments were to be taken with a grain of salt.

At least, Fitz was serious about his wretched fishing. Polly was all too aware that he regarded her painting in the light of a suitable hobby which would naturally fade away when she had her own home and family to care for. Like his sister's watercolours — she had not forgotten his sister. As for Bev, she rather thought he was the quintessential bachelor. She doubted she would be called upon to reject him. Not that she really considered Fitz likely to propose marriage. After all, he was a peer and she was merely the daughter of a sea captain.

Thank heaven they were well-bred gentlemen who would not dream of paying a call before eleven in the morning. She had a couple of hours to herself now. What she really wanted though was the time and the weather to start on another portrait of Kolya. Since Fitz and Bev arrived, she had seen so little of him.

As if in answer to her thought, there was a knock on the door, and he came into the studio.

"Mr. Volkov," she greeted him with delight, "I was just wondering when I should be able to start another painting of you. Are you not going out with Ned this morning? I could make some sketches if you are not in a hurry."

He smiled, but his eyes were grave. "I am not going out with your brother. I have just now taken leave of him, and of *madame* and Nicholas." His voice sounded strained.

"Taken leave? I don't understand." Polly had a horrid feeling that she did understand, all too well.

"I must go today to Brighton."

"That is not far. You are going for several days?"

"I cannot be sure for how long. The king commands my presence."

"The king!"

"Lord John believes His Majesty may offer me a position in his household."

"Then you might not come back?" Polly struggled to keep her voice even. She could not meet his eyes.

"Whatever happens I shall visit the Danvilles."

"So perhaps I . . . we shall see you again one day. I . . . I am glad to have made your acquaintance, sir, and I wish you well."

"Miss Howard!" He held out both hands towards her but she pretended she did not see. He cleared his throat. "Miss Howard, I may ask you one favour?"

"Yes, of course." Surprised, she looked up. For a breathless moment she thought he was going to kiss her, then he stepped back, as if afraid to be too close.

Again he cleared his throat. "I would like to take a few pictures, as reminder of our friendsh . . . acquaintance. You do not mind?"

"No," she said dully. "Take what you want." She realised that her hands were tightly clenched together, and made a deliberate effort to relax them. She wished she had not — they seemed to have been holding her together, and suddenly she felt limp all over. Reaching behind her for her stool, she sat down and stared blindly at her toes.

He did not speak as he sorted through the crates of paintings, and she did not ask which he wanted. She did not even care how many he took.

His firm tread returned across the room and stopped before her. "Thank you, Miss Howard."

"You are welcome, sir." Raising her head, she looked into his face.

Did the regret in his hazel eyes rival her own? No, she must have imagined it, she thought, remembering Lady John's warning, but at least he was not laughing at her. She could not have borne that.

He bowed, awkwardly because of the canvases under his arm, and in a few swift strides he was gone. No word of sorrow at parting, no promise to meet again — the door clicked shut behind him and he was gone. All she meant to him was a light flirtation, a pleasant way to pass the time while he was stuck in the country with no better entertainment. He even expected to forget her without her paintings to remind him.

Polly sat quite still until she heard the crunch of his horse's hooves on the gravel. Then she picked up her paints and lost herself in a fiery sunset of angry reds and blazing oranges.

Three days passed before she checked to see what Kolya had chosen. The picture of Five Oaks was gone, with the apple blossom and another landscape. He had taken a painting of a small boy who had been so fascinated by her one day at the Pantiles that he had stood and stared for a good half hour, until his scolding nursemaid came and removed him. And he had taken his own portrait.

"I wish he had left me his portrait," she said sadly to Ned when he came into the studio after stabling Chipper that evening. She had all her sketches of Kolya spread on the table.

He was shocked. Though Mrs. Howard had told him Polly was pining for the Russian, he had thought it just another of his mother's unwarranted worries. He was always out most of the day, and though he had noticed his sister's quietness in the evenings, he had set it down to her usual abstraction while planning a new painting.

"You put a great deal of effort into painting Volkov," he said with attempted casualness. "It must always be a wrench to part with your best work. Are you coming in now to dress for dinner?"

"No, I have to clean up here first. Don't worry, I shall not forget the time." Her smile was a pitiful travesty of her usual cheerfulness.

Hurrying into the house, Ned found Mrs. Howard in the sitting room, folding her sewing. "Mother, you are right, Polly is in the mopes. I fear she is too fond by far of Mr. Volkov."

"Did I not say so? I was glad when he left, but she continues to fret herself into a decline."

"Is it as bad as that? My poor sister! No wonder you are worried."

However, his mother's anxiety was by no means all for her daughter's health. "The worst of it is that when Lord Fitzsimmons and Mr. Bevan are here she sits in a corner like a mouse and makes no effort to attract them. She will lose them both, mark my words."

"Surely you would not have our Polly setting her cap at those gentlemen! I hope she has better principles than to do any such thing."

"Of course she is not to set her cap — such a vulgar phrase, Ned. I meant only that they were both enchanted with her sunny nature and now the sun is hidden in clouds of gloom."

Ned was unimpressed by his mother's fanciful eloquence. "You cannot expect Polly to put on a show of gaiety when she is unhappy."

"Men are so very impractical," bemoaned Mrs. Howard. "Think how wonderful it would be to see our girl a baroness. Of course Mr. Bevan has no title, but he is related to the best families and able to support a wife in style. It is worth a little effort to catch one of them."

"I believe you are over optimistic. Even if Polly were her usual contented self, I cannot suppose that either his lordship or Mr.

Bevan has any serious intentions. They must be acquainted with scores of young ladies far more eligible than my sister."

"Lady John was a governess," his mother reminded him stubbornly.

"Well, I shall talk to Polly," said Ned with a sigh, "but if she does not have a mind to either I shall not press her. I wish she might find a husband she can care for who is of our own station in the world."

"The world?" Nick bounced in, grubby and dishevelled as always. "I'd give the world for something to eat right this instant, but Mrs. Coates says I must wait until dinner-time. I wish you will put Ella in charge of the kitchen, Mother. She would not starve me half to death."

Reminded of the hour, Mrs. Howard hustled her sons upstairs to wash off their dirt and change their dress. It was too late for Ned to talk to Polly before dinner, though she, for once, was in good time. Sure that the interview would be painful, he wanted to get it over with.

Fortunately, after the meal, Nick took himself off about his own business when his elders repaired to the sitting room. Ned settled his mother by the fire with a branch of candles to light her everlasting sewing. Polly sat at a small writing desk in the window with her sketch book before her. She often spent the evenings planning the composition of her next landscape, but Ned saw that she was gazing out into the dusk without even picking up her pencil.

He hesitated, unsure how to introduce the subject of her suitors. It would be easier, he thought, if he were her father rather than her brother and her friend.

She started as he pulled up a chair beside her and put his hand over hers. "Polly, dear," he said with quiet sympathy, "I hate to see my tranquil, cheerful sister so despondent."

"Despondent? Not I." She smiled brightly.

"I fear you miss Mr. Volkov," he persisted.

"I'm by far too busy to miss anyone, I assure you."

"Then you do not fancy yourself in love with him?"

"In love? Heavens no! Is that what has brought about your long face, dear Ned? Pray put it out of your mind. Mr. Volkov was an agreeable acquaintance and I enjoyed his company, but Lady John warned me, you know, that he is a shocking flirt, so of course I did not take him seriously."

Ned was afraid she was trying to convince

herself, but his relief at her denial was such that he allowed her to persuade him that her heart was untouched. Though she undoubtedly missed the Russian, in time she would regain her serenity. He braced himself to tackle the next point.

"Mother tells me you have lost interest in your aristocratic admirers. Do you dislike Lord Fitzsimmons and Mr. Bevan?"

"I like them very well."

"Then will you try to look more kindly on them? Mother fears you will drive them away, and either would be an excellent match."

"I would never marry a man only because he was an excellent match," she said, indignation overcoming her listlessness.

"I know you would not and I'm glad of it," Ned soothed. "But you said you like them."

"No better than I liked Dr. Leacroft or Mr. Grant."

"Your Tunbridge Wells suitors? I seem to remember the rector of King Charles the Martyr popped the question, too."

She smiled at his teasing, a real smile. "Yes, and I refused them all. I doubt I shall ever marry, Ned, for a husband will expect me to give up painting, and that I will not do."

He believed her. In the weeks she had

lived at Loxwood, he had come to compre-
hend her dedication to her work as he never
had on his short visits to Tunbridge Wells.
She was capable of being a loving, if absentminded, wife and mother, but she would
never have any attention to spare for household matters. The man who married her
must be sympathetic and encouraging as
well as loving, ready and able to relieve her
of the practical details of everyday life.
Where was she to find such a paragon?

Ned sighed. The weeks since his sister,
his mother, and his brother had joined him
had also taught him that he wanted a family
of his own. He wanted children in his house,
a little Nick and Polly who would call him
Papa. He wanted a wife . . . but there his
longing dissolved in formless dreams of
warmth and comfort.

He gave his sister a quick hug and kissed
her cheek. "I'll take care of you, Poll," he
said, and went to try to explain to his
mother why her undutiful daughter intended to refuse the hand of a wealthy
baron. He hoped she would consider that
her rejection of the charming but destitute
foreigner was compensation enough.

Polly had almost succeeded in convincing
herself, with her words to Ned, that Kolya

had been no more to her than an agreeable acquaintance. He was so obliging it was impossible not to like him, and it was flattering to have a gentleman of discernment admire her pictures — and admire them enough to want to keep five. Besides that, he was a romantic figure with his rescue of Lady John and his escape from Russia. But there was no room in her life for romantic figures. She must put him out of her mind.

She turned the pages of her sketch book, studying the drawings she had made of Loxwood Manor, then began to plan the painting she would begin tomorrow.

It turned out to be a perfect day for painting outdoors, cool and still with interesting cloud shapes sailing ponderously across the sky. Nick helped Polly carry her equipment to a gently sloping field overlooking the gardens and the black-and-white Elizabethan manor, framed by trees clad in fresh springtime green.

She had been working for some time when a loud "Halloo!" announced the approach of Lord Fitzsimmons and Mr. Bevan. Dismounting, they tethered their horses to a hedge-maple and strolled across the tussocky grass towards her, doffing their hats.

"Young Nick told us where to find you,

Miss Howard," Bev said. "We came to say good-bye."

"You are leaving?" Polly breathed a silent sigh of relief.

"Back to town tomorrow."

"Not by my choice!" Fitz broke in. "Thing is, Danville's going to be away for a few days."

"Some sort of political nonsense. You could have knocked me down with a feather when he confessed he's looking to stand for Parliament."

"Daresay I ought to take my seat in the Lords one of these days," said Fitz gloomily. "The pater would be turning in his grave if he knew I hadn't done it yet. But you see, Miss Howard," he returned to his explanation, "it won't do for us to stay at Five Oaks with Danville gone. And when he gets back, he and Lady John will be removing to the manor, as you doubtless know."

"Yes, I'm painting this view of the house as a gift for the Danvilles when they come to Loxwood."

The gentlemen moved to stand behind her.

"Very pretty." His lordship sounded dubious.

Polly smiled to herself. The canvas as yet

displayed little more than patches of colour and light. "You flatter me, my lord," she said demurely, adding a touch of blue to a shadow.

"No, no, I assure you. Deuced pretty, ain't it, Bev?"

"Interesting," pronounced that gentleman with a degree of caution.

"Anyway, the thing is, the Danvilles won't want guests while they are settling down at the manor. It will be a few weeks before I can come down again, but I promise you, my dear Miss Howard, I shall return. I don't suppose there's any chance of you coming up to Town?" he added hopefully.

"I fear not, my lord. I am always particularly busy in the summer, since the weather is often fine enough to allow me to paint outdoors. The trees are green, flowers are blooming — indeed, my family complains that I scarcely have time to pass the time of day." Polly hoped he would take the hint that if he returned to Sussex he would not find her at leisure to entertain him.

She knew she had failed when he said with an indulgent smile, "I particularly admire your contentment with country pastimes, Miss Howard. So many young ladies would spend every moment repining for the frivolities of London." He glanced around.

Mr. Bevan had tactfully wandered off and was poking with his riding crop at something in the hedge. Lord Fitzsimmons seized his chance and Polly's hand.

"Miss Howard," he said, slightly hoarse, his handsome face flushed, "you must know how I admire you in every way. When I return I shall have something most particular to say to you. *Most* particular."

Polly tugged at her hand. With a great effort she managed to keep a tremor of laughter out of her voice. "I beg your pardon, sir, but I fear you may find a smear of paint on your glove. Prussian blue, I fancy."

He dropped her hand and stared for a moment in dismay at his pale yellow pigskin glove, then hid the horrid sight behind his back. "Yes, er, um, nothing to signify," he stammered.

"I daresay your man will be able to remove the stain," Polly said kindly. "Tell him to try a mixture of boiled linseed oil and vinegar."

Lord Fitzsimmons looked blank. The notion of advising his valet on how to clean oil paint off leather clearly baffled him. To his obvious relief, Mr. Bevan returned to join them.

"Hedgehog," he said, an ingenious if un- likely excuse for his absence. "I hate to in- terrupt but we'd best be getting along, Fitz old fellow. One or two more calls to pay," he added to Polly. "Servant, Miss Howard."

His lordship bowed and took his leave, re- peating, but with less assurance, his inten- tion of returning to Loxwood as soon as he was able. As they walked away, Polly saw him whip his handkerchief from his pocket and rub surreptitiously at his desecrated glove.

Chuckling, she turned back to her painting.

Her improved mood did not last. She could not help thinking how Kolya, rather than make fatuous remarks about the unfin- ished canvas, would have been interested in her technique.

Try as she might, he would not stay ban- ished from her mind. She was forced to admit that, even though she did not love him of course, she missed him. She did her best to hide her megrims from her family.

Mrs. Howard was delighted to hear that Lord Fitzsimmons had promised to return. The rest of her meeting with his lordship Polly described only to Ned, so her mother did not know that Fitz's resolve had been shaken.

Ned grinned and said, "What a devious way to discourage an importunate suitor."

Several days of fine weather enabled Polly to finish the picture of Loxwood Manor before drizzle once more confined her to her studio. She was drawing a posy of yellow and purple pansies, and wondering how best to paint the velvety sheen of their petal faces, when Nick burst into the room and shook like a wet dog.

"I went down to the Onslow Arms to fetch the post," he announced. "There's a letter for you. The ink on the outside has run a bit in the rain but it looks to me as if it comes from Brighton."

10

Polly doubtfully examined the damp paper. She had never seen Kolya's handwriting, but the address was written in what looked like a feminine hand. Then she brightened as she recalled that the Russian alphabet was different. He might have had someone write it for him.

He might have had some *female* write it for him — but at least he had written. The smudged scrawl in the corner, haloed where the ink had run, definitely said Brighton and she knew no one else there.

"Open it," said Nick impatiently, offering his pocket-knife.

She slit the seal and carefully unfolded the sheet. Her eyes went straight to the signature at the bottom: Lady Sylvia Ellingham.

"Is it from Kolya?"

"No."

"Oh, then I'm going to get something to eat." Nick took himself off.

Subduing her disappointment, Polly read the letter. Lady Sylvia Ellingham had bought one of her paintings, a picture of a child, in a Brighton shop. She wondered if Miss Howard would be so kind as to come and stay with her for as long as it would take to paint the portraits of her two daughters. She suggested a fee of one hundred guineas, but if this was insufficient she would be happy to negotiate.

One hundred guineas! Polly's landscapes had sold in Tunbridge Wells for seven guineas apiece, five for her and two for Mr. Irving. How much had Kolya received for the pictures she had given him?

Not that it mattered. He needed money desperately, and she hoped he had realised a goodly sum. All the same it hurt to know that he had so quickly parted with them, after asking for them as mementos of their friendship. No, he had changed the word "friendship" at the last minute.

Polly forgot that she had been the first to say "acquaintance."

Brooding over their last meeting was pointless, she told herself firmly. She turned back to Lady Sylvia's letter, but even before she reread it her mind was made up. She would go to Brighton. Between new scenes, new faces, and the bracing sea air, her megrims would vanish.

The pansies abandoned, she dashed

through the rain to the house to write to Lady Sylvia.

Mrs. Howard wept and worried. Nick congratulated Polly enviously — she was going to see the sea. Ned, once assured of his sister's determination, borrowed an outdated edition of the *Peerage* from the manor's library and looked up Lady Sylvia Ellingham.

Her ladyship was the daughter of the Earl of Bridgnorth and had married James, Viscount Ellingham, in 1812. Lord Ellingham's country seat was in Warwickshire and he owned a small estate, Dean House, near Brighton. Since the volume was published in 1813, there was no mention of offspring.

Ned assured his mother that Lady Sylvia was the acme of respectability, and Polly diverted her by asking her assistance in packing for a stay of several weeks. Nick carried Polly's trunk down to the Onslow Arms. Two days after the arrival of the letter, in the middle of another wet afternoon, Polly stepped off the stage at the Ship Inn in Brighton.

She had never seen such a confusion of carriages, ostlers, waiters, porters, and travellers. As she looked around uncertainly, a liveried coachman jumped down from the box of a smart landau and approached her.

"Be 'e Miss Howard?" His voice was slow and countrified, soothing, his face creased with smile lines under his dripping hat.

"Yes, I'm Miss Howard," she said thankfully.

"Lady Sylvia sent Oi to pick 'ee up, miss. If 'ee'll just show Oi which be thy boxes, us'll be off out o' this hubbub."

The coachman seemed to have a preference for the quieter back streets, but through the drizzle Polly caught glimpses of fine houses, elegant terraces, and gardens. To her disappointment she did not see the exotic domes of the Pavilion. Nor, of course, was there any sign of Kolya.

The buildings became smaller and more scattered, with fields beyond. They looked new, and a number were under construction. Then the landau turned in at a gateway and stopped before a pretty Queen Anne house. Even in the carriage Polly could smell the purple-blooming wistaria which grew up its brick front and over the roof of the projecting porch.

Ned had warned Polly that she would be in an awkward position, neither guest nor servant. Doubtfully she regarded the stone-flagged porch with its two white pillars and three steps up to the green front door where a brass lion-head knocker gleamed. Ought she to ask the coachman the way to the servants' entrance? Before she could make up her mind, the door swung open.

"So ye found Miss Howard all right and tight, did 'ee, Dick?" called the plump middle-aged woman on the threshold. She wore a black gown and white apron and cap. The housekeeper, Polly decided as she bustled down the steps with a friendly smile.

Dick opened the carriage door and let down the step. "This be my old 'oman, miss."

"Now what sort of an introduction is that?" scolded his wife. "I'm Mrs. Borden, miss, and welcome to Dean House. Her ladyship's expecting you. Put miss's trunk under the porch, Dick, out of the rain, then stable the horses afore ye carry it up. Please to come this way, miss."

"Thank you, Mrs. Borden." Polly picked up her bandbox, stepped out of the carriage, and followed the woman into the house.

The first thing she noticed in the hall was a vase of flamboyant tulips, scarlet slashed with yellow, reflected in the glossy surface of a beechwood half-moon table against the wall. She stopped to gaze at them in delight.

Seeing her interest, the housekeeper said

in an indulgent voice, "My lady grows 'em herself. She's a great one for flowers. I daresay ye'll be wanting to tidy yourself afore ye meets her ladyship, miss. I'll show 'ee your bedchamber and have hot water brought up."

Polly's bedchamber was on the first floor, a pretty room with ivy-leaf patterned chintz curtains at the windows and the tester bed. The floor was polished oak with a large green and gold rug between the bed and the washstand, and a small, warm-toned Vermeer interior hung on one whitewashed wall.

"Just ring the bell when ye're ready, miss," said Mrs. Borden. "Summun'll come to show the way."

The cheerful maid who brought her hot water curtsied and introduced herself as Jill. "Mrs. Borden says as I'm to take care of you while you're here, miss. Is there aught I can get you now? I'll be up to unpack soon as Old Dick brings your trunk." She took Polly's pelisse and bonnet and put them away in the huge armoire.

Polly thanked her and was once more admonished to ring the bell as soon as she was ready to go down. It seemed to be a happy house, she thought, washing her face and hands with the lilac-scented soap she found beside the basin. And so far, at least, she had been treated like an honoured guest. She was glad she had come.

She was seated at the dressing table, tidying her hair, when a soft tapping sounded at the door.

"Come in, she called.

The door inched open and a small, inquisitive face appeared, with brown eyes and long, straight, pale gold hair.

"Are you the artist?"

"Yes. Do come in. You must be one of my subjects."

The rest of the child appeared, clad in a pink frock with deep rose ribbons. "Hallo. I'm Winnie and I'm six." She turned her head and reached behind her. "Come on, Nettie. She's nice."

A somewhat taller girl in blue, with flaxen hair, allowed herself to be pulled into the room. "Curtsy!" she hissed. "And don't call me Nettie! How do you do, Miss Howard. I'm Annette Ellingham, and her proper name is Edwina." They both curtsied, Winnie with a wobble.

"How do you do, Miss Ellingham, Miss Edwina." Polly smiled at the two children. They were very alike but the elder was slim, with the shy look of a fawn, and the younger sturdy, a merry twinkle in her eyes. It would

154

be a pleasure to paint them.

"She's my sister and she's eight," announced Miss Edwina. "She doesn't like being called Nettie, but sometimes I forget. You can call me Winnie, if you like."

A heavy elderly woman, red-faced, appeared in the doorway. "Miss Nettie, Miss Winnie, you'll be the death of me yet. Didn't I tell you to go down to your ma and wait for Miss Howard there? Beg pardon, miss, these scamps move too fast for my pore ole legs."

"It's all right, Nurse, she doesn't mind," said Winnie confidently. "We can show her the way to Mama's sitting room."

"It's quite all right, Nurse," Polly confirmed, earning a glance of gratitude from Annette. "I am ready to go down, and the young ladies shall escort me."

As they went downstairs, Winnie's hand slipped into hers. Half listening to the child's chatter, Polly wondered what Lady Sylvia was like. Judging by the ambiance of the household she was good-tempered. Her love of flowers — and her appreciation of Polly's talent — indicated an eye for beauty. Polly was prepared to like her on sight.

With Annette following, Winnie led her towards the back of the house, pushed open a door, and ran forwards crying, "Mama,

Mama, the lady is here who's going to paint us."

The woman who set down her book, rose from the chaise longue, and put her arm about her younger daughter was about Polly's age, perhaps a year or two younger. Her hair was the exact shade of Winnie's pale gold, but her brown eyes had Annette's diffident, almost apprehensive expression. She wore a morning gown of pale grey silk ornamented with jet beading, and a net and lace *cornette* with a wide white satin ribbon tied beneath her chin.

"Heavens," said Polly, raising her hand to her bare head, "I forgot to put on my cap."

The ice was broken. Lady Sylvia laughed and came forwards with outstretched hand. "I'm so glad you came, Miss Howard. I see my girls have not been behindhand in making your acquaintance."

"No indeed, my lady, they have been most helpful in showing me the way."

"Pray be seated, ma'am. I have ordered refreshments, as I'm sure you must be tired and hungry after your journey. I wish you had given me longer notice so that I might have sent the carriage to Loxwood to fetch you."

"I have never travelled on the stage before. It was very interesting." Polly sat down, fortunately choosing a large chair as Winnie promptly squeezed in beside her. "Such a variety of people, and the scenery was all new to me," she went on, doing her best to put her hostess at ease.

"If you like to walk, there are some superb views from the downs behind the house." Lady Sylvia took a seat opposite her and Annette pulled up a footstool at her mother's knee. "You can see the sea, and the whole of Brighton spread out below you."

"I shall certainly explore. I doubt Miss Ellingham and Miss Winnie will want to sit still for me for more than an hour at a time."

"Do we have to sit *quite* still?" asked Winnie, wriggling. "I'm not very good at sitting still. Nettie — Annette is much better than me."

The door opened and Mrs. Borden ushered in a girl carrying a tea tray laden with cakes and biscuits and neat little sandwiches. Polly discovered she was starving. There had been no time at the stage stop to swallow more than a cup of tea and a slice of bread and butter.

Winnie jumped down from the chair and went to the tea tray. "I'll get you what you want, Miss Howard," she offered. "Do you like samwiches? And macaroons? They're my fav'rite. And there's queen cakes, do you

like them? Mama, will you cut some gingerbread for Miss Howard, please."

She carefully brought the heaped plate to
Polly, and Annette followed with a cup of
tea. Winnie helped herself to a handful of
macaroons and moved to a straight chair,
where she sat munching and swinging her
feet.

As she ate, Polly described her working
method. "I should like to spend a day or two
just sketching the young ladies, ma'am. At
their lessons, at play, whatever they are
doing. Then we can decide how you would
like them posed."

"Oh, I shall leave that entirely to you,
Miss Howard. I am enchanted by your picture of the little boy."

Lady Sylvia indicated the wall to her right
and Polly saw the solemn, wide-eyed child
she had painted at the Pantiles. Kolya had
chosen well — properly framed and hung it
was indeed charming. She hoped he was enjoying the proceeds of the sale.

The momentary cloud was dispersed by
Winnie, who said hopefully, "Do you want
to see the nursery and the schoolroom? I'll
show you."

"When Miss Howard has finished her tea,
I expect she will want to rest," her mother
intervened.

"I am quite restored, thank you, my lady. I should like a tour if Miss Winnie will oblige. I hope you will go, too, Miss Ellingham?"

Annette nodded, her face solemn as the boy in the picture, then came to perch on the edge of the chair next to Polly's. "Please, ma'am, will you call me Annette? Miss Ellingham doesn't sound like me."

"Certainly, if you will call me Miss Polly."

The child smiled. "Oh yes, that's a pretty name."

Her sister rushed over and thrust her hand into Polly's. "Me too," she said anxiously. "Can I call you Miss Polly, too?"

"Of course."

"Annette, pray bring me Miss Polly's cup to refill, and while she is drinking it, take Edwina to wash her hands. We shall come up to the nursery presently." As soon as the girls were gone, Lady Sylvia said with an air of relief, "I'm so glad they like you. We have few visitors, and I was afraid they might be difficult."

"They are delightful children, and it will be a pleasure to paint them, ma'am," Polly assured her.

Praise of her daughters was obviously the way to her ladyship's heart. Her smile of pleasure increased her likeness to Annette.

159

"Doubtless they will want to show you all their little treasures when we go up," she said, "and then, if you should like it, I will show you mine. My father-in-law was something of a collector, and there are a number of fine pictures in the house."

Polly was delighted. She had had little opportunity of studying the old masters except through prints, which were unsatisfactory at best.

The late viscount, she discovered, had been a connoisseur of Flemish works, landscapes with windmills silhouetted against wide skies, portraits of ordinary people, and intimate interiors like that in her chamber. There were few of the grand Italian paintings beloved by most English collectors, but maybe he had hung those at his main seat in Warwickshire.

By the time Lady Sylvia had shown her every picture in the house, inviting her to examine them later at her leisure, Polly was beginning to wonder where the present viscount was. There had been no mention of him, no references by the girls to "Papa." Nor, she realised, had she seen any menservants except Dick Borden. Though the house was not large and its furnishings were far from ostentatious, everything was of the best. Clearly the Ellinghams were wealthy, and wealthy households, she was sure, were usually run by a butler and boasted swarms of footmen.

The sun was making fitful, watery appearances between the clouds, and Lady Sylvia invited Polly to stroll on the terrace at the back of the house. She forgot about the viscount's absence as she surveyed the brick-walled garden, breathing the scent of heavy-headed lilacs.

Near the house flowers abounded: beds of roses with swelling buds, tulips and pansies, fragile columbines, polyanthus, and rich-hued peonies. Lady Sylvia pointed out a hedged enclosure concealing the vegetable garden. Espaliered fruit trees grew against the south-facing wall, and a huge chestnut, covered now with candle-spikes of bloom, shaded a stretch of velvety lawn. A swing dangled from one branch.

That would be a good place to sketch Annette and Winnie, Polly decided. She might even paint them on the swing.

Beyond the far wall rose the smooth green humps of the South Downs. Polly noticed a door in the wall. "Is that the way to the views of the sea you mentioned?" she asked, pointing.

"Yes. It is locked, but I shall show you where the key is kept in the potting shed. I am no great walker — nor is Nurse, as you may have noticed! — but one of the maids sometimes takes the girls out rambling. If you ever want company I'm sure they would be delighted to go with you."

"How far can one walk on land belonging to Dean House?"

"No farther than the garden wall, I fear." Lady Sylvia seemed ill at ease, but explained, "The estate used to stretch for some distance to the south, but the land has been sold. I daresay it will soon all be built on, for Brighton is growing at a prodigious rate." She dismissed the subject with apparent relief. "Shall we go in? I told Mrs. Borden we shall dine at seven, but if that does not suit you it can be changed."

"I should not dream of upsetting your arrangements, my lady. I expect Lord Ellingham has definite ideas about the dinner hour. My brother Ned is sadly discomposed if he is forced for some reason to alter his habits, though Nick is ready to eat at any time."

Lady Sylvia flushed. "I . . . Lord Ellingham . . . I daresay I ought to have told you that I am a widow."

Contrite, Polly reached out to clasp her hand. "No, why should you? I'm so sorry."

"Indeed, there is no need . . ." Her ladyship was flustered. "That is, it was several years ago. You must be surprised that I do not have a companion, but I cannot think it necessary, living here retired as I do. If I lived in London, or at Westcombe — that is an estate near Lewes I inherited from an uncle . . ."

"I'm sure it is perfectly acceptable for you to live without a companion," Polly said firmly. "Pray do not think that you owe me any explanation."

As she changed for dinner, Polly confessed to herself that in spite of her words she was curious about Lady Sylvia's unusual situation. Her curiosity faded when she discovered that the window of her bedchamber looked out over the garden to the downs beyond. She took her sketch book from the dressing table, where Jill must have put it when she unpacked, and began to draw the flowing shapes of the rolling uplands.

Time passed unnoticed. The maid had to be sent to summon her to dinner.

That evening she wrote a brief note to her family to announce her safe arrival, and a few days later she sent a letter describing her activities. Mrs. Howard gave it to Ned when he came home in the evening.

He scanned it quickly and would have liked to discuss Polly's news over dinner, but the meal was interrupted by a fierce dispute between his mother and his brother. Ned had to order Nick to hold his tongue, an expedient he thoroughly disliked. After dinner, Nick retired sulkily to his chamber, while Mrs. Howard walked down to the vicarage to join in an evening of sewing for the Poor Basket.

Ned went to his office, intending to go over some figures relating to a copse that was to be thinned and the timber sold. He found himself thinking of Polly instead. Until she left he had not realised to what extent her equable temper had acted as a shield between his argumentative brother and his easily agitated mother. Her simple presence, without any active intervention, was a calming influence on both. Ned missed her on his own behalf too. He was aware of an emptiness, a dissatisfaction with his life, which he had never been conscious of before.

He took her letter from his pocket and read it again. She was enjoying herself sketching Lady Sylvia's daughters and beginning on their portraits, walking on the downs, making a thorough study of the pictures at Dean House. She was already grown very fond of both the girls and their gentle mother.

Did he imagine a certain wistfulness when she mentioned that she had had no occasion to go into Brighton, or to view the Royal Pavilion? Ned hated to think that she was still pining for the Russian.

Slowly he folded the letter and put it away in a desk drawer. The figures he ought to be working on stared up at him. A cup of coffee would clear his head, he thought.

He was in the hall on the way to the kitchen when the front door-knocker sounded. Hearing the kitchen door open, he called to Ella, "I'll see who it is."

He opened the front door. On the step stood Kolya Volkov.

11

Ned Howard stared. Kolya could not tell from his face whether he was pleased or annoyed, or simply surprised, to see his erstwhile pupil.

"I beg pardon that I disturb you so late."

"Not at all." His response appeared to be automatic rather than heartfelt but he stood aside and said, "Won't you come in? Your business in Brighton is finished?" He led the way into the drawing room.

"No, I must return tomorrow." Kolya glanced around the empty room. His impatience was not to be contained. "If you please, I may see Miss Howard?"

"Polly is not here."

"I will wait, unless is better I come back in the morning?"

"She's not out, she has gone away. I'm surprised no one mentioned it at the manor if they knew you were coming here."

Limp with disappointment, Kolya dropped into the nearest chair. "I have not been yet to manor. She is gone? To where?"

Ned avoided his question. "Will you take a glass of brandy? Or coffee, perhaps; I was about to have some."

"Coffee, thank you." He waited while Ned rang the bell and gave Ella the order. The maid curtsied to Kolya with a nod and a smile. She, at least, was glad to see him.

"You said you have not been to the manor yet," Ned said abruptly. "Have you dined?"

"*Na samom delye* — as matter of a fact — no."

"There's some cold pigeon pie, sir, and Mrs. Coates could heat up the rest of the sparrowgrass soup."

"Ask her to do that, Ella." His duty as a hospitable host carried out, Ned seemed to relax.

"Please, where is Miss Howard?" Kolya ventured to repeat."

"She has been commissioned to paint a portrait."

His unwillingness to say where Polly was suggested the answer to Kolya. "In Brighton?"

Ned's affirmation was reluctant.

"Already! Is better than I hope. You will give me the address, please? I wish to pay my respects."

"I'll have to think about it. You must understand that my only concern is for my sister's welfare."

Kolya conceded temporary defeat. "I will come in the morning," he said philosophically, and proceeded to enquire about various matters concerning the Loxwood estate.

When, an hour or so later, he rose to leave, Ned said, "You will find that Lady John is still much occupied in organizing her new household. I know you will be welcome at the manor, but she was not best pleased when Lord Fitzsimmons appeared a day or two ago."

"Fitz came back?" Nor did the news please Kolya. "Is not my business, but I beg you will tell me, you gave Miss Howard's address?"

"No," said Ned shortly, sighing. "I shall see you tomorrow."

Kolya rode on to the manor, well fed and in good spirits. Ned Howard was a good fellow, and their parting had definitely been more amicable than their meeting. Besides, he had a plan. If Polly's address was still withheld in the morning, he would suborn Nicholas. The lad was bound to know the name of his sister's patron if he did not know the address.

John and Rebecca Ivanovna were happy

to see him. They sat up late discussing John's plans to stand for election to Parliament. Nonetheless, they were all at breakfast when Ned Howard arrived at the manor at nine the next morning.

Ushered into the dining room by the new butler, the nephew of the stately individual who had tyrannized over the Five Oaks staff for decades, Ned accepted a seat and a glass of ale. He apologized to Lady John for introducing business at her breakfast table.

"My lord," he continued, "I mentioned to you the necessity of finding a buyer for the timber which is to be cut down. I have heard that Mr. Nash, the architect, is purchasing materials for building the king's new chapel at the Brighton Pavilion, and it occurred to me that, being so close, we might make an advantageous sale."

"Sounds like a good notion." His lordship cast a knowing glance at Kolya. "You'll want to go down to Brighton, I daresay, to make arrangements. You will stay at his Grace's house, of course."

"Thank you, my lord. I wondered whether . . . that is, do you suppose it would cause any difficulty if I took my brother with me?"

"I doubt one more will seriously disrupt the household. Want to keep your eye on young Nicholas, do you?"

"He's a good lad, sir, and I wouldn't want you to think otherwise. It's just that, well, my mother's nerves are not of the strongest . . ."

Kolya and John laughed. "I seem to remember when I was that age her Grace never set eyes on me without suffering a spasm," said John understandingly. "By all means take the boy."

"I shall call on Mrs. Howard while you are gone," Lady John promised, "to make sure she wants for nothing."

"Thank you, my lady, you are very kind." Ned looked at Kolya.

"We shall travel together, of course," Kolya assured him. His heart was light. The cautious brother would not be going to Brighton to keep an eye on his sister if he did not mean to reveal her whereabouts. "I am at your service."

Ned had a few matters of estate business to deal with before their departure, but travel was swift on the fine June day. It was shortly after four by the time the three reached the outskirts of Brighton and walked through the gates of Dean House.

"Why can't I wait till tomorrow to see Polly?" Nick demanded, not for the first time. "If I'm going to join the Navy, the sea is *much* more important."

"The sea will still be there tomorrow," Ned pointed out.

"So will Polly." Heaving a big sigh, Nick abandoned the argument as his brother raised the gleaming door-knocker.

"I'm Miss Howard's brother," he told the maid who opened the door. "Pray inform her that I am here."

She looked flustered. "I'll 'ave to ask Mrs. Borden, sir," she said, and scurried off.

They waited several minutes on the door-step, Kolya increasingly impatient, Nick muttering remarks of which "waste of time" were the only audible words. At last a grey-haired woman approached.

"Miss Polly's out, sir, but if you'll step this way her ladyship'll see you in the garden."

Kolya had no desire to meet her ladyship, but politeness forbade retreat. Apparently agreeing wholeheartedly with the first part of this reflection, Nick stepped backwards. Kolya seized his arm and propelled him after his brother. In the wake of the house-keeper, they crossed the hall and a sitting room to emerge through French doors onto a terrace.

Far from strolling the walks of the garden, or taking her ease on one of the benches scattered about it, Lady Sylvia was on her knees by one of the flowerbeds, planting out seedlings.

"Here's Mr. Howard, my lady," Mrs. Borden announced.

Her ladyship cast a quick, scared glance up at them from under the wide brim of her hat, then returned to her task with dogged determination. As Ned went down the brick steps towards her, Kolya held Nick back. If for some reason the pretty young woman was afraid of them, it was better if she had only one to deal with.

Kolya heard her say in a hurried, breathless voice, "You are Miss Howard's brother?"

He could not make out Ned's words, but his tone was soothing. A moment later he helped Lady Sylvia to her feet and with her returned towards the terrace. Her steps were slow and reluctant.

"It seems Polly has taken the Misses Ellingham for a walk," Ned said. "Her ladyship has kindly offered to show us which way she went, if you choose to go with me, Volkov?"

"Not I," murmured Nick, but he had manners enough to keep his comment inaudible to all but Kolya.

"Certainly," Kolya assented promptly. A

meeting in the countryside would suit him much better than in a drawing room.

Ned presented his companions to Lady Sylvia. As she turned to lead the way across the garden, Kolya saw her appealing look at her housekeeper, who was still standing on the terrace. Mrs. Borden gave her a nod of encouragement.

Though Kolya was mildly intrigued by this odd behaviour, his mind was on Polly. He and Nick followed Ned and the lady through a door in the wall around the garden. Immediately beyond, a chalky path ran at an angle across a gentle slope of short, wiry turf to a stile set in a hedge wreathed with blush-pink dog roses.

When they reached the stile, Lady Sylvia stopped. On the other side the path divided into three and the slope steepened, rising unbroken to a rounded hilltop. She pointed to the right-hand path.

"Miss Howard said she was going to go that way."

Kolya had the impression that she meant to return to the house, but Ned offered his arm to help her over the stile. She accepted it without demur, and without looking at him.

After a few minutes at a slow pace behind her ladyship and his brother, Nick drew level and said, as if expecting an argument, "I'll go on ahead. Can you see the sea when you get round the side of the hill, ma'am?"

"I'm not sure. Possibly."

That was enough for Nick, who set off at a brisk walk. With a word of apology, Kolya hurried after him.

The view to the south turned out to be blocked by another rise. Nick was disappointed. Kolya was not — at the far end of a valley filled with a tangle of bushes and what looked like the ruins of a house, he saw three figures: a woman and two girls. He grinned as he noticed the rectangle of a sketch book under the woman's arm.

"There is your sister."

Disappointment forgotten, Nick bounded ahead, yelling and waving. "Polly! Hi, Polly!"

Kolya was tempted to follow suit, but the dignity of his years forbade it, if only because Ned and Lady Sylvia would appear around the bend at any moment. His stride lengthened, however, and he was not far behind Nick when brother and sister met. He saw Polly's glad welcome, and saw her expression change to one of wary reserve as she turned to him.

Nick interrupted her stiff greeting. "Can you see the sea from the top of this hill?" he asked.

Polly looked blank. The smaller of the two children answered. "Yes, come on, we'll show you." She took Nick's hand and tugged.

He looked startled but said, "All right."

"Come on, Nettie."

"We have to ask Miss Polly," the older girl reminded her.

"Yes, go on," Polly said distractedly. "Take care of them, Nick."

Kolya's unexpected appearance seemed to have sent her wits a-begging. She had recognized him from a distance and joy had flooded through her, but face to face with him she could find nothing to say. The hurt of knowing he had sold her pictures returned.

His smile had become a look of puzzled concern. "You do not mind that I have come?"

"No. No, of course not. Ned gave you my direction?"

"He brought me here. I have something for you." He plunged a hand into his pocket and pulled out a roll of papers. "The flimsies, they are called. They are yours. I sold two pictures."

"Money? For me?" A surge of relief dizzied her, and she put her hand on his arm to steady herself.

His warm, strong hand covered hers. "You are pale. You must sit down."

"I'm quite all right," she protested, but she allowed him to spread his coat on the dry, springy grass and sat down. A scent of crushed thyme arose.

He sat on the fragrant turf beside her. "I did not mean to give a shock. I thought you knew. Did not Lady Sylvia buy one painting?"

"Yes, she has the one of the little boy." Polly was ashamed of having doubted him. Everything she knew of him should have told her that he was incapable of being so underhanded as to sell her work for his own profit.

"I wanted you to know that even in Brighton, where the king has many art treasures, your painting is valued," he explained. "Here, take this money. Is seventy guineas after shopkeeper has taken a share. It is enough?"

"It is more than I could ever have hoped for. But I do not need it, sir, and you do. You must keep it."

"I take lady's money?" His outrage made her even more ashamed. "Did I not tell you when first we meet that I will not take lady's money?"

"Just the shillings in the guineas? As a commission?"

"Nothing." He smiled, and she realised he was teasing her. "You have so kind heart, but you must not worry for me now. My father is not permitted by the tsar to send me money, but he asked Prince Lieven, the Russian ambassador, to lend. He gave to me when he came last week to see the king, and my father will repay in Russia."

"I'm very glad you have heard from your family."

"Is no kind message." Kolya produced a rueful grimace. "My father is almost so angry as tsar, but will not let the son starve."

"You have enough to live on?"

He shrugged. "Is not a great amount, but I am a guest of the king so my expenses are not high. You like my new coat?"

Polly jumped up. "You mean I'm sitting on a new coat? I assumed it was one of the ones Lord John gave you."

Laughing, he reached up and pulled her down. "Will not be damaged if you keep the feetwear off it. Is meant for outdoors, not for king's drawing room."

"Have you seen the king?" She recalled his reason for coming to Brighton.

"Not yet. His Majesty is ill with fear that the Privy Council will allow Queen Caroline to be crowned with him. In Russia, when the emperor wishes to dispose of his wife, he imprisons her in a monastery. Perhaps English way is more civilized, but is less efficient."

"Our Henry VIII managed to dispose of six wives."

"Six!" Kolya sounded admiring.

"Well, five, strictly speaking. Divorced, beheaded, died, divorced, beheaded, survived. Poor George did not even succeed in divorcing one."

"She makes him very unhappy. Even Lady Conyngham cannot cheer him."

"Have you met Lady Conyngham? What is she like?"

"She is handsome woman for her age, but not, I think, clever. I have met many people since I came to Brighton, but you I have never seen in the town."

"I have not been into town since I arrived. Lady Sylvia is something of a recluse. Oh heavens, here she comes! Where has Nick taken the girls?"

Once again Polly jumped up, and scanned the hillside opposite. Just below the crest were three small figures, the smallest somewhat higher than the other two. She heard a faint whoop and saw Winnie race down the steep slope to be caught by Nick and whirled around.

"Remember Susie Stebbins?" she said

laughingly to Kolya. "Little girls seem to like Nick. But then, Winnie is not one to stand on ceremony."

"And the mother seems to like Ned," he responded, shaking his coat and putting it on. "Lady Sylvia was — how shall I say? — the timid, milky water miss when we came."

"Milk-and-water." Polly turned and saw that Lady Sylvia was leaning on Ned's arm and conversing with more animation than she had hitherto displayed.

As if conscious of their gaze, her ladyship looked up and blushed, letting go of Ned's arm. Ned waved, and Polly and Kolya went to meet them.

Hugging her brother, Polly said over her shoulder, "I let the girls go with Nick up the hill, Lady Sylvia. I hope you do not mind. They will be back at any moment."

She looked anxious, until Ned said, "He will take care of them, ma'am. Polly, you look very well."

"I am." Suddenly she felt like laughing with happiness. The world was a wonderful place that June afternoon.

"Her ladyship tells me your portrait of Miss Ellingham is nearly finished," Ned continued.

"Yes, it is going very well." The laughter within her escaped. "Winnie is another matter. The poor dear finds it so very difficult to sit still."

"Sit still!"

For a startled moment Polly thought the shout of exasperation was a peculiar echo. Then she recognized Nick's voice and swung round with the others. Winnie's hatless, golden, tousled head appeared above the hazel bushes in the valley, moving towards them. Of Nick and Annette there was no sign.

"He carries her on the shoulders," Kolya suggested.

His guess proved correct a few minutes later when the trio emerged from the thicket. Annette, neat as when she had started out, carried her sister's hat in the hand that was not tucked confidingly into Nick's.

"That's a bang-up place for hide-and-seek," he announced, swinging the little girl down from her perch.

"Mama, may we play hide-and-seek?" demanded Winnie. "Nick will show us how."

"Not today," said Lady Sylvia, putting her daughter's hat back on the tangled tresses and tying it firmly under her chin. "It grows late. But perhaps if you ask him very politely, Mr. Nicholas will come back one day to play with you."

Nicholas looked appalled.

"*Please,* Nick? I promise I will not call you Nicky."

He glanced down at Annette.

"If you please, Mr. Nicholas," she said in her shy, grave way, "if you are not too busy looking at boats, will you come and visit us again?"

He heaved a deep sigh, then grinned and said, "Yes, I'll come. I'll bring a spyglass, and we shall go up to the top of the hill again and look at boats from there."

As they all walked homeward, Kolya said to Polly, "If you ask me very politely, I shall come and visit you again. Or rather, I wish to show you the sights of Brighton. Is shocking that you have not seen the Pavilion."

"I should like to."

"You know it is not yet completed? After thirty-four years, still is scaffolding and rubble and more plans, always changes. I have talked to many people who are not pleased, because that they have not been paid for work, or because that the mess spoils their business for many years. The house where I stay is to be demolished, if the king can persuade the owner to sell."

"I hope they will not knock it down until you have moved out!"

"I think not. The king has never enough

money to make things as he wishes. I tell you this so that you are not disappointed. Even unfinished, the Pavilion is an impressive sight."

"I suppose you cannot show me the interior?"

"But of course. I have friends who will allow although the king is in residence. Is much of interest to an artist and also, I warn you, much that is in the vulgar taste."

"I want to see it all," said Polly.

12

The dining table at Dean House could have accommodated twenty. Polly was used to dining with Lady Sylvia, just the two of them, but that evening after her brothers and Kolya had visited, the room seemed empty. She thought of Lady Sylvia sitting there alone, night after night, and her heart went out to the lonely young woman.

"I hope you did not mind Ned bringing Nick and Mr. Volkov to call," she said, as a maid departed after replacing the remains of a roast chicken and peas with a bowl of gooseberry fool.

"Not at all. I was a little taken aback at first — you know I rarely receive visitors. I hope they did not think me rude?"

"Ned told me you were most obliging." A gentle, pretty creature he had added, but Polly was not going to repeat that.

"Mr. Howard impressed me as a sensible gentleman, and . . . and remarkably agreeable. I have never met a gentleman before who treated me as a real person, not as a fool

183

or as just one of his belongings, there for his convenience."

"I know what you mean. Lord Fitzsimmons wants to marry me, but he sees me as a . . . a sort of amusing ornament. Not all men are like that, though."

"No, some are much worse. I daresay you have wondered why I live so retired." Lady Sylvia stirred her dish of pudding with a nervous gesture, then pushed it aside.

"You do not have to explain to me," Polly assured her.

"I want to. You see, my experience of the world, and of men in particular, has not been happy. I was only seventeen when I married, and not by my choice."

"Your family's choice?"

"My father forced me to marry Lord Ellingham. He was forty, more than twice my age, and even I, though I led a sheltered life, knew of his reputation as a . . . a rake and a libertine, but he was excessively wealthy and Papa had debts."

"And your mother?"

"She said it was my duty to the family."

Polly thought of her own dear mama, who might worry and fuss but would never try to force her to do anything that would make her unhappy. She took Lady Sylvia's trembling hand in hers.

"My brother wanted to go into the army, and my sisters wanted their Seasons in London. How could I stand in everyone's way? But oh, Polly, you cannot imagine how dreadful it was." Tears of remembered anguish trickled down her cheeks.

"Come into the drawing room, you cannot have a proper cry at table." Polly put her arm about Lady Sylvia's shoulders, helped her up, and steered her through to the next room.

They sat together on an elegant green brocade sofa, her ladyship sniffing into a tiny lace-edged handkerchief. Polly pulled a large, fortunately clean, paint rag from her pocket. "Here, take this. How long was it before the wicked ogre died?"

Lady Sylvia summoned up a tremulous smile. "He was killed in a duel three years after we were married, just after Winnie was born. Though he had sold all the Dean House land by then, to pay his gambling debts, not long before the duel he won a vast sum, so he left me wealthy. My family wanted me to go back home, but I refused."

"I don't blame you a bit!"

"His family blamed me for not bearing a son and heir, and for not reforming him, though how they expected me to do that I cannot guess. So you will understand that I have little contact with either family. I was used to think myself perfectly happy alone here with the girls and the garden and my books, but since you came I have realised that something was missing."

"Companionship. I'm not much of a companion, I fear, always busy with my pencil or brushes, or off in another world planning what to do next."

"Oh no, you have been just what I needed. If I wanted someone forever hovering about me, I could have taken a paid companion, as everyone urged me to do. The only thing is, I have no one to turn to for advice."

"If there is anything I can help you with, you know you have only to ask."

Lady Sylvia hugged her. "I know. Your coming to paint the girls is quite the best thing that has happened to me this age. But I doubt the subject is one on which you are any more knowledgeable than I. It is a problem concerning the estate."

"The Ellingham estate in Warwickshire? Was it not entailed to the new viscount?"

"Yes, it went to a distant cousin, which is one reason the Ellinghams were displeased with me. It is Westcombe that concerns me. You may remember I mentioned that I had inherited a small estate from an uncle? He was the only person who sympathized with me, and he left Westcombe to me so that I should never be quite dependent on my husband."

"I remember. It is near Lewes?"

"Not fifteen miles from here. The girls and I generally go to stay for a month or two in the summer." She frowned. "For two years or more the revenue has been declining, and now someone wants to purchase the estate. My bailiff and my solicitor both advise me to sell, but neither will explain matters to me because I am a woman. They are probably right, I should not understand if they did, but I refuse to run to my father for advice."

"Of course not. You must ask Ned."

"You think he would not mind?"

"I'm sure he will be pleased to help. He is the kindest of brothers. And being a land agent, he will know just what's what."

"That is what I thought when you told me his profession, but I should not have dared to ask before I met him. He did seem kind, and . . . altogether amiable. If Ellingham had been like Mr. Howard . . . Well, I can see that not all married women are to be pitied, after all."

The next afternoon, Polly was in the garden sketching a moving target — Winnie being pushed on the swing by Annette — when Kolya was announced. Hat in hand he came running down the steps from the terrace, made his bow to Lady Sylvia, who was sitting on a nearby bench, and turned to Polly.

"I have borrowed a phaeton and a pair of horses," he announced. "Do not wish to interrupt, but perhaps my lady will be so good to excuse you for tour of Brighton?"

"Ten minutes," said Polly. The sight of his tall, lithe form made her slightly breathless, but Winnie was cooperating for once and she was determined to finish her drawing.

Though Kolya, as expected, was amused rather than offended by the delay, Winnie, as might have been expected, was unable to sit still when a visitor had arrived.

"Is Mr. Nick coming today?" she called eagerly.

"Not today," Kolya told her. "I introduced Nick to my friend who is fisherman, and he was invited to go today in boat on the sea. Also I have a friend who is retired naval officer who will tell him stories of Navy. But Nick has not forgotten you. He asked me to tell you, will come tomorrow to play the hide-and-seek."

"Then may I go today with you and Miss

Polly?" Winnie jumped off the swing without waiting for it to stop and landed on hands and knees. Looking at her hands, she screeched, "Mama, there's blood!"

As Lady Sylvia hurried towards her wailing daughter, she said to Polly, "You had best go at once, before she recollects that she wants to go with you. Enjoy yourself."

Polly hesitated, but Annette ran up and said earnestly, "You need not worry about Winnie. She is not hurt. Seeing blood always makes her cry."

So Polly and Kolya slipped away. The borrowed carriage turned out to be a high-perch phaeton, its body slung between huge wheels. It was a very smart crimson and black vehicle drawn by a coal-black pair.

"You are not nervous?" Kolya enquired, driving through the gateway and turning left towards town.

"Nervous?" Polly was surprised. "Why?"

"Some people consider high-perch phaeton is a dangerous carriage."

"Nick has told me you are a top sawyer, and while I am aware that you have told him any number of tall tales, I do not believe you would exaggerate your skill. Besides, we shall have a splendid view of everything from so high above the ground."

"You are never afraid, I think."

"I suppose fear seems to me a singularly useless emotion." She pondered a moment and then went on, "If I thought you would overturn the carriage I should not be here with you, so there would be nothing to be afraid of. Having accepted the ride, being afraid would not prevent an accident."

That made him shout with laughter. "Is very practical view of life," he admitted.

Since her mother frequently accused her of impracticality, Polly was pleased. She glanced up at him, to find him grinning down at her with a light in his eyes that made her wonder whether perhaps she was a trifle nervous, after all. Quickly she looked away, and gave a cry of delight.

"Is that the Pavilion?"

Before them spread an enchanted palace of oriental domes and spires and minarets, lacy screens of carved stone, pillars, arches, and cupolas. Kolya pulled up the horses to let her stare at leisure.

"I have to paint it."

"But of course. You can wait a little while?" he enquired politely.

"Wait? Oh, you are teasing again. Yes, I shall have to wait, for I did not even bring my sketch book. Besides, I want to see the rest of the town, but can we drive right around the Pavilion first?"

As they circled the grounds, Polly was silent, studying the different façades from different angles. She could not help but notice the stacks of bricks, stone and timber, the heaps of rubble from half-demolished houses, the workmen with wheelbarrows and handcarts shouting as they scurried through the dust and din of hammers and saws. For thirty-four years, Kolya had said, this place had been a construction site.

"No wonder the neighbours are disgruntled," she said as he pulled up again at the original spot.

"Disgruntled?"

"Upset. Vexed."

"Disgruntled," he repeated. "Is good word. Yes, I have spoken with many such. Is Mr. Wright, a teacher of music, who was supporting wife, eight children, and two sisters with the lodging house and subscription library, but people will not go to his house because of noise and dirt. He wrote letter three years ago asking for help, and still he has no answer. Also Mr. and Mrs. Shergold, and Dr. Hall, whose patients will not come, and many others. Some are more than disgruntled — are very angry."

"Who can blame them?"

"I have promised to present new letters directly to the king when I see him. I doubt if others ever reached him."

"That is kind of you. I wonder whether I could set up my easel on a pile of stones, so as to have a clear view."

"*Nyet!* This I forbid!" Kolya's vehemence startled Polly. "I beg your pardon, I have not right to forbid, but I beg you will not. If stones are not . . . *ustoychivy* . . ." He snapped his fingers in annoyance at his inability to find the word.

"Stable? Steady?" she supplied obligingly.

"*Da*. Steady. Is too dangerous. You have no fear but I, I admit, I have fear for you."

"Very well, I will not. I shall just have to pretend the mess is not there."

He reached across and pressed her hand, then started the horses off again. "*Spasibo*. Thank you. Now we shall drive on the Steyne. You can explain this name?"

This time Polly was unable to oblige. The Steyne was simply a wide open space used as a promenade. The Pavilion would front it on one corner once all the houses that obscured the view were demolished. The Castle Tavern, with its assembly rooms, a number of fine houses, and many circulating libraries, book shops, and printsellers surrounded all but the southern side.

Kolya pointed out the printseller who had sold Polly's pictures. She wanted to see if he would take the two panoramas she had painted of Brighton from the downs, but she decided to postpone a visit in favour of going to look at the sea.

As they drove across the Steyne, they were hailed several times by riders, strolling pedestrians, and the occupants of other open carriages. Kolya seemed to know a vast number of people, both ladies and gentlemen. To some he just waved, but he stopped once or twice to introduce Polly. They had nearly reached the Marine Parade when a plump, handsome woman in an elegant barouche signalled imperiously and Kolya drew up alongside.

"Good day, Mr. Volkov." The lady's bonnet sported a display of plumes of which an ostrich might have been proud, and diamonds sparkled at her neck and ears.

"Good day, Lady Conyngham. Allow me to present Miss Howard."

The king's favourite, her eyes suddenly sharp and inquisitive, bowed graciously. Polly returned the bow. A few remarks were exchanged on the fineness of the weather and Lady Conyngham drove on.

"I felt that I ought to curtsy," said Polly as

Kolya set the horses in motion, "but I was not sure how to do it without oversetting the carriage. Her ladyship is very affable."

"Her ladyship is wondering are you related to the Duke of Norfolk. Howard family is one of oldest in the country, I understand. The vice-queen, as she is known, is a daughter of London shopkeeper and the wife of obscure Irish lord. It pleases her to hobble-nobble with ancient nobility." The scorn in his voice surprised Polly almost as much as his rare mistake delighted her.

"Hob-nob, but I like hobble-nobble much better." She glanced down at her plain and far from new gown of dark blue cambric and rubbed guiltily at an overlooked streak of brown paint. "She cannot possibly have mistaken me for a relative of the Duke of Norfolk. I expect she was surprised to see anyone so dowdy being driven by you in such a smart carriage."

Kolya laughed. "On contrary, she thinks you well-connected eccentric. Before her stands dilemma; Lady Conyngham is of the religious mind, and Howards are powerful Catholics. Is dangerous to offend yet she cannot approve."

"I would not have her worry for nothing. Promise you will assure her that I am not related."

"She will look down the nose at you," he warned.

"I'm not like to meet her again, and if I do what does it matter what she thinks of me?"

"Does not matter," he agreed, giving her a smile so warm it made her cheeks grow hot.

By this time they had reached the Marine Parade. Polly forgot her loss of composure as she gazed at the smooth, dark blue swells of the English Channel.

"Sea is colour of your eyes," Kolya murmured, but it was easy to ignore his disconcerting words with such a prospect spread before her.

Scattered fishing boats rose and fell as the waves rolled shoreward beneath them. Where the water met the sand below the shallow cliff it spread in a lacy froth with a constant susurration, a murmuring background to the mewing cries of the grey-winged gulls that circled above.

"What are those odd huts on wheels?" Polly enquired. "Look, a horse is pulling one into the sea."

"Those are the bathing machines, for changing of clothes. Watch and you will see a person come out and go down steps into the water. The king first came to Brighton in youth for the sea bathing, for his health. I have heard he was too bold and one of dippers had to stop him going into stormy sea."

"That woman helping the person down the steps, she is a dipper? Oh, look, she is swimming!"

"You wish to try?"

Polly watched the shivering swimmer emerge from the waves with the aid of her dipper and hurry back into the machine. "Not unless the water grows a good deal warmer," she decided. "I expect Nick will want to try it. Oh, you said he is gone out on a fishing boat? I wonder which one?"

They watched the boats for a few more minutes, then Kolya drove her through the old part of town, pointing out the area known as the Lanes, too narrow for the carriage, where the fishermen lived. Here too he was known, saluted by old men mending nets and nodding to the women who curtsied as the phaeton passed. He stopped to pass the time of day with a ship's chandler who stood in the doorway of his bow-fronted shop, his thumbs hooked into his braces.

"You know everyone!" said Polly. "You have only been here a week or two."

"I like people," he said simply.

On the way home they passed the Pavilion again, and Polly began to plan the pictures she would paint of it. Lost to her surroundings, she was surprised when they pulled up in front of Dean House.

"*Thank* you," she said as Kolya helped her down from the high seat. "That was a bang-up tour, as Nick would say. Will you come in for tea?"

"I think not today."

"Lady Sylvia will not mind."

"This I know. She is already your friend — is she not? — though you have been here only a week or two."

"I like people, too," she explained, smiling.

"Is good." He kept her hand in his though she was safely down. "However, I must return carriage. You permit that I come tomorrow to hobble-nobble with you?"

Polly laughed. "Oh yes, do come and hobble-nobble." Again she thanked him, and watched as he sprang up into the phaeton. He drove off with a flourish, looking very dashing, and she turned and went slowly into the house.

He liked people — of course that was good, but did it mean that she was just one among the many people he liked? She consoled herself with the thought that at least, among so many others, he had time to spare for her.

13

The next day, Kolya arrived at Dean House on foot, accompanied by Ned and Nick. Ably seconded by Winnie, Nick requested permission to take the girls to play hide-and-seek. This was granted, with the proviso that they stay away from the ruined house. It had been gutted by fire some years since, Lady Sylvia said, and much of it was still standing, but it was unsafe. Nick promised to steer clear of the place and went off with Winnie hanging babbling on his arm and Annette walking soberly alongside.

Kolya suggested to Polly that they should walk into town to take her paintings to the printseller. Knowing that Lady Sylvia was hoping for a private word with Ned about her estate, Polly agreed.

"I had best go with you," said Ned, frowning. "It cannot be proper for you to go about the streets alone with a gentleman."

"I will send a maid," Lady Sylvia said promptly, then blushed. "She can carry your paintings. But indeed I do not think it necessary for propriety, if you are to walk in the main streets which are full of company. Brighton is by no means so strict as London in that regard."

So Kolya carried the canvases, which the printseller was delighted to accept on commission. Mr. Lay, whose mother had had a print shop in the very same spot on the Steyne for many years, turned out to be another friend of Kolya's. A small, tubby man, he had the face of a good-natured gnome. While Polly was examining his wares, displayed in two small, crowded but well-lit rooms, he and the Russian had their heads together in intimate discussion, the subject of which Kolya did not mention as they strolled back to Dean House.

They found Ned and Lady Sylvia also with their heads together in intimate discussion. Nick brought her daughters back shortly thereafter, and Winnie invited the gentlemen to stay for nursery tea.

Adding her invitation, Lady Sylvia proposed moving this repast to the dining room for the nonce. While this suited the gentlemen much better than the nursery chairs, Winnie disappeared behind the table, even with a cushion beneath her. She tried kneeling, decided that was uncomfortable, and slid down. She went to stand beside Ned.

"I can't reach properly," she told him. "Can I . . . May I sit on your lap? If you please, sir."

Polly was surprised by Ned's gratified expression as he pushed back his chair and lifted the little girl to his knee. He proceeded to stuff her with every sweetmeat within reach.

Annette seemed overawed by the company. She watched wistfully as her bolder sister chattered to Ned, then turned to Polly, sitting beside her, and confided in a whisper, "I like your brothers."

"I'm glad."

" 'Specially Nick. He never calls me Nettie even when he's teasing. He said he hates being called Nicky so he understands."

She looked across the table at Nick as she spoke. He grinned and winked at her. "Annette found quite the best hiding place this afternoon," he announced. "Of course it helps that she stays still and quiet as a mouse. Winnie always giggles."

"That's 'cos I want you to find me," Winnie explained, and beamed complacently when all the adults laughed.

Sitting on the terrace that evening in the long June twilight, Polly asked Lady Sylvia whether Ned had been able to advise her about the sale of Westcombe.

Her ladyship looked abashed. "I did not get around to asking him," she confessed. "We were walking in the garden, talking about gardening, and then about books, and somehow the time passed and you returned. He is so very easy to talk to, I quite forgot my problems. I have not had a serious conversation with a gentleman before, for Ellingham cared nothing for my interests."

"Ned is always ready to enter into the interests of others, even painting, about which he knows little enough in all conscience. I told you how he had a studio already prepared for me when we arrived at Loxwood."

"He makes me think I have quite misjudged the masculine half of humanity, though the examples I knew were sufficient to mislead me. Do you think he will call again?" she asked anxiously.

"I'm sure of it, even if I go home. I have finished the portrait of Winnie, you know, and have no more claim upon your hospitality."

Lady Sylvia was dismayed. "But I thought you wanted to paint the Pavilion. I was looking forward to having you stay at least a few more weeks. Must you go?"

"Well, no. I hoped you would say that." Polly grinned disarmingly. "Mama seems to be perfectly happy with her friends, Ned's business is taking longer than he expected, and I *do* want to paint the Pavilion. I shall not even suggest that my presence might inconvenience you, lest you should agree."

"Never! I wish you may paint a dozen pictures of the Pavilion."

Polly started on the first of the proposed dozen the next morning. As usual she began by sketching the scene, setting up her easel where she had a view of the east façade between the piles of building materials. Within minutes she was surrounded by children, and as they drifted away their parents came to see what she was doing.

At frequent intervals she had to blow away the dust that settled on her paper.

"Aye, miss, 'tis dirty right enough," said a harassed-looking woman who had just arrived. "Many a year we've been living with it and no heed paid to our letters."

"It must have made your lives excessively difficult," Polly commiserated.

"Difficult!" broke in another woman. "My Jack's business has been ruined and the children hungry, nor ever a penny's compensation have we seen."

A man had joined the group, decently dressed but shabby, with a twitching nerve in his thin cheek. "There's them as won't put up with much more," he said. "I've heard talk . . ."

"Hush your mouth, Albert," said the second woman abruptly. "Miss don't want to hear your rumour-mongering. That's a right nice picture you're making, miss."

"Better hurry up and finish it," the man advised, "or it may be there won't be nothing left to draw."

The two women hushed him and hurried him away. Polly wondered for a moment what the man had meant, but she soon forgot his words in the fascination of the intricate architectural details of the Pavilion.

She had been sketching single-mindedly for an hour or so when Kolya came out of the nearby building he was staying in. He joined her just as she was once again dusting her drawing.

"How you will paint with all the dust in the air?" he enquired, greeting her with a smile. "Does not matter so much for a sketch, but with the oil paints will make terrible mess."

"Yes, I had not thought of that. I shall have to paint at home, from sketches." She frowned. "Perhaps if I come in the evening they will have stopped work."

"But here on east side light will not be good in the evening, I think."

"I shall just have to paint several pictures, as Lady Sylvia suggested. One at home, and one of the west front, and perhaps one here with the domes silhouetted against the sunset."

"Lady Sylvia has invited you to stay?"

"As long as I wish. Is it not kind of her?"

"I am glad. I must go into the Pavilion now, to see if is chance to see the king today. This afternoon I come to Dean House."

The days sped past. Polly was too busy and too happy to note their passing. One wet afternoon Kolya took her and Ned and Nick to see the interior of the Pavilion. As he had told her, much of the furnishing and decoration was elegant and tasteful, with odd touches of fantasy like the couch in the form of a Nile riverboat standing on crocodile legs. The Music Room, however, was extraordinary beyond her wildest imaginings.

The walls were painted with Chinese scenes in gold on red panels. Each panel was framed at the top with *trompe l'oeil* depictions of fearsomely realistic dragons and serpents. The chimney-piece was another dragon, carved in white marble, and porcelain pagodas stood at intervals along the walls. Beneath their feet strange monsters writhed across the blue carpet.

Polly became aware that Kolya was watching her. She was afraid that if she caught his eye she would laugh aloud, and there were several other people in the room.

"Even the pelmets have dragons and snakes," she said weakly.

"And the chandeliers." Nick was enthusiastic. "Ned, can Polly paint my bedroom at home like this?"

That was too much even for Ned's gravity. Kolya, his shoulders shaking silently, hurried them out amid affronted stares.

It was two days later that Ned decided he needed to go to Westcombe in order to be able to advise Lady Sylvia properly.

Polly was up on the downs overlooking Brighton, working on a new panorama of the town. Nearby, the girls were running down the slope to be caught by Nick and whirled around. Even Annette was breathless and laughing, though she did not squeal with delight like her little sister. When they saw Ned coming, they ran to meet him.

He caught one in each arm, kissed their cheeks and continued up the hill to Polly, hand in hand with both. Polly could not remember ever seeing him so carefree.

Sending the children back to Nick, he sat

on the grass beside her and explained the need to investigate Westcombe in person.

"If something dishonest is afoot," he went on, "then the bailiff must be involved. The trouble is that if I go alone he will be suspicious. Lady Sylvia cannot go with me without a respectable female to play propriety. You're elected, Polly." He grinned at her.

"But I cannot go now. I'm in the middle of this, and of the Pavilion paintings. Surely you can find someone else? Send for Mama."

"Asking her to do anything so out of the ordinary would only distress her unnecessarily. Besides, it will be good camouflage to have you paint a picture of Westcombe. It will provide a reason for my being there."

"Oh Ned, I'm sure you can manage without me. Suppose the weather were to change before you are ready to return, so that I cannot paint outside." Polly tried to persuade herself that her reluctance had nothing to do with the fact that Kolya would not be there.

"Apart from anything else, you can scarcely stay on at Dean House in the absence of your hostess. It will be for only a few days, and the weather could change tomorrow anyway," he pointed out with unassailable logic.

Logic won the day. That afternoon when Kolya arrived, Polly told him that servants had been sent ahead to Westcombe to prepare the house. He seemed unconcerned that she was going away, merely wishing her a pleasant visit. In fact, he appeared to be more interested in Ned's explanation of the problems with the estate.

Polly could not help wondering whether he had only been squiring her about from a sense of obligation. Doubtless he was tired of escorting so unfashionable a lady in this fashionable town.

The following afternoon the Howards and the Ellinghams reached Westcombe in time for tea. Despite her megrims, Polly was glad of an opportunity to paint the house. A Tudor half-timbered building, not unlike Loxwood Manor though somewhat smaller, it nestled in a fold of the downs, framed by the steep, sheep-cropped hills.

Immediately after tea, Winnie and Annette took Nick off to explore the house. Polly went outside to begin planning her painting, the purpose of the visit already half forgotten.

She scarcely saw Ned for the next few days. When he was not out talking to neighbouring farmers, he was buried in the Westcombe accounts or closeted with Lady Sylvia, presumably discussing his findings. Polly knew he had ridden into Lewes, for he made a point of telling her it was a charming town, worthy of her brush. When she finished her picture of the house she thought of requesting a carriage to take her there, but then she went walking with Nick and the girls and discovered the view from the top of the hill behind the house. The steep northern slope of the downs fell away into the Vale of Sussex, opening new vistas which demanded to be painted.

One warm evening, warned by her stomach and the westering sun that dinnertime was approaching, Polly carried her equipment down the hill to the house. Entering by a back door, she passed the small room Ned had been using as an office. From it came an angry bellow.

"And who the bloody hell are you to jump down my throat!"

Ned's voice was crisp and clear. "As I told you, Mr. Welch, I have her ladyship's authorization to act in her name."

"I'll just have a word with her ladyship meself."

A slight movement in the dim passage beyond the door caught Polly's eye. Lady

Sylvia, looking frightened, was backing away. Polly went to her, missing Ned's next words, but the whole house must have heard Mr. Welch's response.

"Dismissed! I'll see you damned in hell for this, Howard, and her bloody ladyship needn't think I'll take it lying down neither. You'll both of you regret this day's work."

Lady Sylvia was shaking. Polly put her arm round her waist and led her away. A backward glance showed Dick the coachman, elderly but sturdy, coming in through the back door. He winked at her, looking not at all discomposed, and she recalled catching a glimpse of Mr. Welch a day or two before. The overseer's voice was more impressive than his short, stout frame.

Old Dick stopped at the office door. "Will Oi be a-sendin' fer t'magistrate, sor?" he enquired.

Polly heard no more. The hall was full of chattering maids who fled as she led Lady Sylvia to the drawing room. The housekeeper bustled after them, tut-tutting.

"Tea for her ladyship if you please, Mrs. Borden. Or no, better a glass of wine I believe."

"Edward . . . Mr. Howard . . . will he be all right?" Lady Sylvia said faintly. "I never should have asked him . . ." She burst into tears.

"Ned can take care of himself," Polly assured her.

By the time she had soothed the distraught woman, Ned was entering the drawing room. Far from appearing fearful, he was positively jaunty.

"That's all settled," he said with satisfaction, then noticed Lady Sylvia's pale, tear-stained face. "Syl— Ma'am!" In three strides he was on his knees before her, taking her hand. "I promise you, ma'am, the wretch is gone. You have nothing to fear. It is settled."

"What I should like to know," said Polly placidly, noting with interest her ladyship's trembling smile, "is just what has been going on at Westcombe."

Ned stood up and took a seat opposite. "It's a bit involved. You know that the greater part of the estate is down in the Vale of Sussex?"

"Is it? I have been painting the view on the other side of the hill, but I have to admit I did not know who owned it."

"I don't suppose you did," he said indulgently. "Be that as it may, there is an adjoining estate in the valley, Wivelston Place, which is selling off two or three farms. The house itself is not for sale, so the price is good. It seems her ladyship's solicitor in Lewes has amassed quite a fortune, by what means I prefer not to know, and had a notion to set up as a country gentleman. He has an option to buy the farms but he wanted more than that, so he conspired with our friend Welch to persuade Lady Sylvia to sell."

"As I must have done in the end, had Mr. Howard not discovered the plot." Hands clasped, Lady Sylvia leaned forward with an earnest expression and continued, "I must reward you for your assistance, sir, or at least pay you for your time and trouble."

"That is not necessary," said Ned brusquely, rising to his feet.

Though taken aback she persisted. "I have dared to hope that you might agree to take the position of bailiff here at Westcombe."

"Impossible. As it is, I have wasted too much of my employer's time. I must ride to Brighton tonight to conclude Lord John's business there in the morning, and then return at once to Loxwood. Polly, I trust you and Nick can be ready to leave Brighton by noon."

"Impossible," said Polly, noting that her brother looked everywhere but at Lady

Sylvia. "I cannot guarantee even to be in Brighton at noon tomorrow, and if I was I have a dozen things to do there."

"But . . ."

"I'm sure Lady Sylvia will be willing to let Nick stay at Dean House, so you need not be concerned at leaving him alone at the duke's."

Her ladyship, bewildered, nodded acquiescence.

"As you will," said Ned, impatiently. He bowed to Lady Sylvia. "Thank you for your hospitality, my lady. I shall look out for someone suitable for the vacant position."

A moment later he was gone. They heard his hurried footsteps in the hall.

"I did not mean to offend him." Lady Sylvia's brown eyes once more swam with tears. "I have come to rely on him."

"I am sure he will always be willing to advise you."

"It is not just his advice I want," she wailed. "Somehow his presence is so very comforting."

To Polly's relief the girls came in to say good-night, forcing their mother to regain her composure. Then it was time to change for dinner. Polly caught Nick before they went down and told him of Ned's departure. His surprise was short-lived; he was much too eager to describe a bang-up afternoon spent haymaking with a new friend to worry about the doings of his elders.

At the dinner table, his chatter diverted attention from Lady Sylvia's low spirits and lack of appetite. Immediately after dinner her ladyship retired, claiming a slight headache. Polly was left wondering why Ned should take offence at the offer of a job, and why Lady Sylvia was so out-of-reason upset by his sudden departure.

They all returned to Brighton the following afternoon, in time for Polly to go straight to the Pavilion to paint. Kolya found her there, in her usual spot, and asked how the visit to Westcombe had gone. Always lively, he seemed full of suppressed excitement, his slanting eyes sparkling as he listened to her uncertain answer.

"Very well, I suppose. Ned discovered that the bailiff and the solicitor were in league to cheat Lady Sylvia — only that leaves her without either."

"I daresay are some very good solicitors in Brighton. I will find one, and he will find a new bailiff, *nyet?*"

"Yes, I should think so. That is excessively kind of you." He shrugged. "Is nothing. I wish I knew already enough to take position for self. But soon at least I return to studies."

Polly had been going to tell him about the contretemps between her brother and Lady Sylvia, but this comment distracted her. "You have seen the king at last?" she demanded.

"Yes, I have seen the king. Is most affable gentleman. And I have done more — I showed to the king your pictures, and His Majesty has bought two."

Polly stared, dazed. "Mine? My pictures? The king bought two of my pictures?"

Kolya nodded, grinning. "Wait, is more. When I saw the king, already I have arranged with Mr. Lay to hold an exhibition of your work. And when I told this to the king, he gave leave to claim that the exhibition is under the Royal Patronage of His Majesty, King George the Four."

14

"And Mr. Volkov is going to take me tomorrow to make final arrangements with Mr. Lay." Far too excited to care what she ate, Polly helped herself at random from the dishes set out on the white cloth.

"It is excessively obliging of Mr. Volkov to go to so much trouble for you," said Lady Sylvia, summoning up a smile. Her subdued and inexplicable unhappiness was the only check on Polly's joy.

"I think you ought to marry Kolya," Nick proposed, piling his plate high with mushroom fritters and succulent slices of roast sirloin. "He's a great gun."

"He has not asked me. Besides, he is a gentleman, and we have no real claim to gentility."

"Kolya is not so stupid as to care for that. He has friends of every station."

"Friends, yes, but a wife is another matter."

"Forgive me for meddling in what is none of my concern," Lady Sylvia said earnestly, "but I believe you rate yourself too low, and Mr. Volkov too high. It is not as if he is a nobleman, only a private gentleman and a foreigner, and your father was an officer."

"Mama is forever pointing out that Papa was an officer," Polly agreed with mingled doubt and hope.

"It is not an insuperable gulf, where there is true affection." Her ladyship blushed painfully. "But of course I cannot say . . . I do not know . . . I beg your pardon!"

"Nor do I." Polly sighed. "In any case, he is not in a position to marry, and though I have earned more than I ever hoped, I cannot possibly support a family."

"This exhibition of yours will make a fortune," Nick prophesied. "Then you can buy that estate next to Westcombe and hire Kolya to manage it on condition that he weds you."

His sister laughed at his triumphant expression, but Lady Sylvia looked sadder than ever. Marriage was not a topic calculated to cheer her. Polly changed the subject.

She tried not to place too much importance on Lady Sylvia's belittlement of the difference in station between herself and Kolya. Nonetheless, ever the optimist, she woke in the morning with hope added to the thrill of the prospect of her own exhibition. Sooner or later Kolya would be able to support a wife, and if he asked her she would wait for him.

Even if he did not ask her, she would probably wait for ever, she acknowledged with a rueful smile at her image in the glass.

She was glad she had never got around to wearing a spinsterish cap, but her wardrobe was sadly shabby and outdated. Should she spend some of her money on a new gown or two?

She was still pondering this question when Kolya came to fetch her, this time in a borrowed curricle. Though he stigmatized his team of high-stepping roans as "showy slugs," the phrase pleased him greatly. His spirits were as high as Polly's, and everything they saw as they drove into town was a source of amusement.

As they passed the Pavilion, Polly remembered that he had promised to present letters from the distressed neighbours to the king. She asked if he had done so.

"Yes, I gave them to His Majesty, but I fear he will do nothing. At present he can think of nothing but his feud with the queen. He passed the letters to equerry, and they will no doubt go to Mr. Nash, the architect, who already cannot pay bills of builders."

"So I suppose the builders are angry, too. I wonder the king can sleep at night when he owes money to so many people."

"I believe he does not sleep well, but for worry over Queen Caroline, not over debts."

"If his mind is so taken up with his wife, I daresay he did not offer you a position?"

"On contrary, he offered a commission in the Guards. I will not take, however. Is not good, I think, to be in the army of the country that is not my own. But do not fear, I now know many people of influence and wealth. When I have learned all that Ned can teach, I will not have difficulty in finding post."

They turned onto the Steyne. A moment later he halted the showy slugs in front of the print shop and tied them to the railing. The proprietor came out to greet them. Beaming, he ushered them into his establishment and led the way into the inner room, lit by skylights.

"You see, I have already begun to clear the space," he said, waving his hands at one wall almost bare of pictures. "It's quite a job, finding somewhere to put them, I can tell you. Now, ma'am, how many pictures was you reckoning on hanging? Mr. Volkov said a couple of dozen. We don't want to crowd 'em, you know, like they do at the Royal Academy."

"I can provide twenty-four or so. I expect Lady Sylvia will lend hers. You have some way of marking those that are not for sale, I daresay?"

"To be sure, ma'am, to be sure." Mr. Lay rubbed his hands. "I've taken the liberty of drawing up a handbill. It's all ready for the printer's, saving the date. If you'll just step back this way, ma'am, sir, I'll show it you and you can tell me any changes you want, and we'll fix on a date that suits."

From under his counter, he produced a roll of paper and spread it on the polished wooden top.

Mr. Adolphus Lay
respectfully begs to inform
his illustrious clients
of a private EXHIBITION of paintings
the work of
Miss Howard
at his premises on the Steyne
under the GRACIOUS PATRONAGE of
HIS MAJESTY KING GEORGE IV

Polly read it in awed silence. Kolya frowned.

"This 'Miss Howard,' " he said. "Must

be . . . how do you say *'glavnaya bukva'*?"
He pointed at the bottom line.

"Capital letters? If you say so, Mr. Volkov, but it'll have to be smaller than the king's name."

"And why private?" Kolya asked. "We wish that many people come."

"Aha, now that's a little trick of the trade, if you get my meaning, sir. Invite the public and the nobs'll stay away. What you do is invite half a dozen Names as people recognize — Lady Conyngham, f'rinstance, who'll be flattered to be asked to the opening — then you pass the word who's coming and sell tickets to them as wants to be seen with the Names. Then after a day or two you publish another bill for the public and they all flock to see what the nobs was so interested in."

"That sounds very clever," Polly marvelled.

"I'll tell you what would be clever, miss. If Mr. Volkov can borrow them paintings the king bought, now that'd bring 'em in like flies to a honey-pot."

"I will ask," Kolya promised. "I will go on the knees and beg."

They settled on the ninth of July, a week hence, for the opening of the exhibition, then Polly and Kolya went out to the curricle. As he was handing her in, Lady Conyngham's barouche pulled up alongside.

"Good day, Miss Howard," she said condescendingly, her plumes nodding. "I expect you are making arrangements for your exhibition? His Majesty is delighted with the paintings Prince Nikolai sold him."

"Thank you, my — Prince Nikolai?" Polly stared at the vice-queen.

She tittered. "Oh my, don't tell me he has not mentioned it to you! The king did say it was in confidence, but I presumed, as you are such great friends, that you would know his true rank."

"True rank, my lady?" Her heart sinking, Polly turned her gaze on Kolya, standing beside the curricle, who appeared distinctly embarrassed.

"Why yes, Miss Howard. Our mutual friend is Prince Nikolai Volkov, eldest son of the tsar's minister of state. Gracious, I see I have set the cat among the pigeons. You must give His Highness a good scolding, my dear. Drive on, James."

Kolya looked up at Polly pleadingly. "Am not highness. Highness is only imperial family."

Feeling betrayed, her hopes withering,

she looked straight ahead. "But you are a prince."

"Yes. My father is Prince Volkov, tsar's minister. In Russia are many princes."

"If not highness, what should I call you?"

"Excellency is correct word, but I wish that you call me Nikolai Mikhailovich, or Kolya." He reached towards her. She did not turn her head and he let his hand drop. "Even Mr. Volkov is better."

"Pray drive me home at once, Your Excellency."

"Polly . . ."

"Or I shall walk."

She made as if to climb down and he hurried to unhitch the roans from the post. Inside she was crying, but her eyes were dry, burning. When he sprang up beside her, she edged away from him, pressing against the side of the curricle.

"Miss Howard, let me to explain," he said urgently.

"What is there to explain? You deceived me. You deceived us all."

"Because that I feared you will be vexed."

"You were right. Your Excellency."

Stiff and silent he drove her home. When he stopped in front of Dean House she jumped down without waiting for his help and hurried into the house.

No wonder his eyes were always laughing, she thought savagely. He was laughing at her gullibility.

Avoiding everyone, she fetched her sketch book and hurried across the garden, through the door in the wall, and up into the hills. The harebells were in bloom, their delicate blue flowers nodding in the breeze. There were purple knapweed, the tiny pansy-faced heartsease, yellow rock-rose and pink field bindweed. She would draw a peasant's bouquet and be damned to princes.

Nick found her there. He was alone, his spyglass under his arm, a bounce in his step as he strode towards her.

"Where were you earlier, Poll? I was looking for you. A letter came from Ned: the duke has got me a midshipman's berth! On HMS *Steadfast*. Is it not famous?" He stood with his hands in his pockets looking down at her.

"Famous! I'm excessively happy for you, Nick, dear. Does that mean you are to leave at once?"

"Not right away. She's outfitting at Tilbury docks. Ned's going to take me up to London on the seventeenth, and we are to stay at Stafford House while all the papers and stuff are completed and I get my uniform. I'd rather stay here till then. There aren't any ships at Loxwood."

"The seventeenth?" The exhibition was to open on the ninth of July — if the exhibition was still to be held. Without Kolya's — the *prince's* — support Mr. Lay might be unwilling to proceed, Polly thought dismally. All her plans and hopes were crumbling around her.

"You don't sound very happy," said Nick dubiously.

Polly tried to smile. "Indeed I am very glad, though we shall all miss you horribly. I'm a little tired, I think."

"Better come home and have some tea," he advised, helping her to her feet. "That will make you feel better."

She kissed his cheek before he could duck. "You sound just like Mama. Tea, the sovereign remedy."

"Actually, I was thinking of sandwiches and cakes, not tea to drink. Lady Sylvia has a bang-up cook."

Lady Sylvia's bang-up cook, having grown accustomed to Master Nicholas's insatiable appetite, provided a gargantuan spread at tea-time. The drawing room being no place for this feast, Nick and the girls would guzzle to their stomachs' content in the dining room, while her ladyship and

Polly contented themselves with delicate porcelain cups of tea in ladylike seclusion.

On fine days the ladies repaired to the terrace, and Polly found Lady Sylvia there. They sat and sipped in mournful silence for several minutes.

A blackbird's warble drew forth a heavy sigh from Lady Sylvia. "I fear my megrims are affecting you," she apologized. "I had hoped rather to catch your cheerfulness."

Polly echoed her sigh. "I was thinking of your words last night."

"I do not recall saying anything to make you unhappy," she said anxiously.

"On the contrary. You gave your opinion that the gulf between Mr. Volkov and myself was not impassable. Today I learned that far from being a private gentleman, he is a prince."

"A prince?" gasped Lady Sylvia. "You are roasting me."

"No, it's true. I'm not roasting you but he has been deceiving me — all of us — all these months. He is the eldest son of one of the tsar's ministers."

"How did you find out?"

"I must suppose that the Duke of Stafford told the king, asking him at the prince's request to keep his true identity secret; the king let it slip to Lady Conyngham and she, whether from spite or simple lack of discretion I cannot guess, told me. How he must have laughed in his sleeve to see us accepting his friendship as sincere!"

"You do not think . . ."

"He cannot have meant it. A prince does not choose his intimates among such simple country people as we. I am ashamed of the way we tried to lay claim to gentility." Unable to sit still, Polly jumped up and went to lean against the balustrade, staring out blindly over the garden.

"But you *are* gentlefolk," Lady Sylvia insisted.

"Not I." She laughed bitterly. "Gently bred young ladies do not take up oil painting and sell their work, nor do gentlemen . . . Forgive me, I did not mean to burden you with my humiliation. I must go and paint the Pavilion while the light lasts."

Her forehead wrinkled, Lady Sylvia watched her go, realizing she had been going to say that gentlemen do not earn a living overseeing other men's estates. Mr. Volkov — the prince — had talked of becoming a land agent. Polly must believe that was simply more deception on his part.

She was so sure that her birth made her unworthy of him. Did her brother see life from the same perspective? Lady Sylvia wondered if Ned thought friendship with her as impossible as Polly thought it with the prince. If so, he must have considered her offer of a job as an unsubtle reminder of his inferiority. How stupid, how insulting she had been!

She had not meant it so. She wanted him for a friend, an adviser, a . . . No! That she dared not admit even to herself. She went in to see what her daughters were up to.

Polly did not return for dinner.

"It's not like my sister to miss a meal," Nick observed.

"She was distressed. I expect she lost her appetite."

"I thought she was not quite her usual self. Do you know what is wrong, ma'am?"

Lady Sylvia explained about the unmasking of Kolya Volkov.

"A real prince?" said Nick. "That's famous! Girls do get upset about peculiar things." He proceeded to plough through a huge meal as if he had not devoured a substantial tea a few hours since.

However, by the time he was satisfied the sun had set and even Nick was beginning to be concerned.

"I know it will be light for an hour yet," he said, "but I think I ought to go and see where she's got to, don't you, ma'am?"

"Oh yes, please do, Nick," said Lady Sylvia, relieved. "She said she was going to paint the Pavilion."

"Right you are. I'll bring her home safe and sound, never fear." He went off whistling.

15

Polly's gaze was fixed unseeingly on the Pavilion. For the first time in her life, she found it difficult to concentrate on her work. The thought of Kolya's deception nagged at her. She could not believe she had actually let herself dream of the possibility of being his wife.

He was the first man she had met who had actually encouraged her painting. She had had no fears that as her husband he would insist on her dropping her work to take care of family responsibilities. Of course, why should His Excellency, Prince Nikolai Mikhailovich Volkov, care whether an obscure Englishwoman gave her life to her art or to household duties? It made no possible difference to him.

His kindness in arranging the exhibition was doubtless simply a matter of *noblesse oblige,* of the obligation of the aristocracy to patronize the arts. Her hostility on discovering his identity had probably killed that patronage. She ought to have pretended she did not care, for the sake of her work.

But she did care. She had not wanted to marry him because of his support, but because she loved him.

The castle in Spain had crashed to the ground. Before her stood the palace in Brighton, waiting to be painted. She must not let her foolishness destroy her dedication. The sunset behind her bathed the pale Bath stone and white-painted domes in rosy light, glinting on windows. All was still; the workmen had packed up their tools and departed to their homes.

Polly scraped off the paint hardening on her palette and mixed a fresh batch. For half an hour she worked steadily, till the last of the pink tint had faded from the walls though the western sky was still streaked with crimson.

She was packing up her equipment when she saw a file of men moving through the dusk towards the Pavilion. There were six of them, four carrying small barrels on their shoulders. They seemed to be dodging stealthily from shadow to shadow between the brick piles and bushes, heading towards the south end of the building. Polly watched them, puzzled by their odd behaviour.

As they disappeared into a group of trees, a cheerful whistle announced Nick's arrival.

"You missed dinner," he said by way of greeting.

"The light was just right. Look, Nick, do you see those men?" She pointed to where they were emerging from the trees.

"What about them?"

"They are behaving strangely. They have been sneaking up to the Pavilion as if they do not want to be seen."

"It does look as if the one in front is scouting the way and the last man is guarding the rear. Do you think they are burglars?"

Polly tried to calm her brother's excitement. "Surely not. Why would burglars be carrying barrels? I expect after all they are just delivering kegs of brandy or something. The kitchens are at that end of the building."

"A wine merchant's men wouldn't be skulking in the bushes," Nick said scornfully. "Come on, we'd best go see what they are up to." He set off at a run.

After a brief hesitation, Polly followed at a more sober pace, abandoning her painting things. She could not leave Nick to investigate on his own, whether the men were on legitimate business or some sort of skulduggery.

Since Nick, like his quarry, dodged from

cover to cover and she went straight towards the corner where the six had last been seen, they arrived at the same moment to see the rear guard sneak into the Pavilion by a small, inconspicuous door. Nick pulled her behind a bush as the man glanced round suspiciously before closing the door.

"I know him," Polly said. "That is, I have seen him before. He owns one of the lodging houses on the other side of the Pavilion."

Nick made a dash for the door. He put his ear against it, paused, then tried the handle. He beckoned urgently, and Polly joined him.

"We cannot go in!" she objected.

"Yes we can, it's not locked. It's our *duty* to find out if they are burglars." Forestalling further argument, Nick pushed the door open a crack, peered in, and slipped inside.

Decidedly uneasy, Polly went too.

They were in a narrow passage. From ahead came kitchen smells and the sound of voices. There was only one door onto the corridor, on their right.

"They must have gone through there," Nick whispered, "or they would have been seen."

"I expect they went straight ahead and delivered their barrels of flour to the cook," said Polly hopefully, but Nick was already testing the nearby door. To Polly's dismay it also was not locked.

An oil lamp hanging on the wall illuminated a flight of brick steps leading down into a wine cellar. The air was chilly. Rack after rack of bottles, some gleaming, some coated with dust, stood like silent sentinels in serried ranks.

"I told you it was brandy."

"Sshh, they're not in here. Come on."

Polly was amazed at how softly Nick could move when he tried. They made their way past the wine racks till they came to a cleared aisle. To their right it led to a row of doors where the width of the cellar appeared to be partitioned into several rooms. To their left it led under brick arches into the dim distance.

"There!" breathed Nick, pointing.

For a moment a figure was clearly outlined against a pool of lamplight, before it vanished again into the shadows.

Creeping from arch to arch, they passed rows of hams hanging from the ceiling, huge tuns of ale that scented the air with hops, stacks of barrels marked Cognac and Madeira, and then a long stretch of black heaps of coal. Here and there stairs lit by lamps provided access to the unseen magnificence above their heads.

As they approached the far end of the cellar they passed an extinguished lamp, and then the last one ahead of them winked out. Once again Polly was ready to turn back, but Nick grabbed her hand and tugged her after him into the darkness. She did not dare protest aloud.

A spot of light bobbed across a row of doors like those at the south end some four hundred feet behind them, reached the last to the left and found the lock.

"Dark lantern," Nick whispered.

A hand came out of the darkness with a large key, inserted it in the hole, and turned. The lantern moved into the room. Against its faint glow they saw four silhouettes follow. A fifth stood in the doorway, his tense pose suggesting he was alert to hear the slightest sound. Polly held her breath.

Moments later the lantern reappeared, the key once more clicked in the lock, and the six men came towards them. The barrels were gone.

Nick and Polly scurried back from the aisle and huddled behind a brick pier as they approached. They moved stealthily, in single file, always keeping to the shadows. For several minutes after they passed, the watchers stayed in their hiding place.

"Bloody hell," swore Nick softly. "How

can we see what they are up to when they locked the door?"

Polly refrained from reproving his language. "It must be something nefarious. Let us get out of here and go and tell someone."

They slipped back the way they had come, staying well behind and out of sight of the villains. When they emerged into the corridor at the top of the stairs, Polly turned towards the kitchens.

"Where are you going?" Nick demanded. "It's no use telling the scullery maids. We must go and find Kolya."

"Kolya! Oh no!" Despite her words, Polly followed him out into the night. The palest tinge of pink still remained in the west, and she recalled her abandoned equipment. "I must fetch my easel."

"All right, but then we'll go to Kolya. I know you are upset because he's a prince, though I'm dashed if I can see why, but he's still *my* friend and he will know what to do."

Kolya was not at his lodging. They went to the Pavilion's main entrance and asked for him. The bewigged footman in his scarlet livery looked down his long nose at Polly's paint smock and the coal dust on her hem and informed them in no uncertain terms that Mr. Volkov was not on the premises. When Nick tried to explain that they had seen men with barrels behaving in a suspicious manner in the cellars, he snorted and said, "Run along now, sonny, afore I calls a guard."

As they turned away, they heard him mutter to his fellow, "Barrels in the cellar, what next! Bats in the belfry if you ask me."

Disconsolate, they walked homeward under a rising moon. "I suppose we are making a mountain out of a molehill," Polly said hesitantly.

"They were not behaving as if they had legitimate business there. Unless the king buys smuggled brandy and has it sneaked into his private cellar." Cheered by this thought, Nick resumed his jaunty whistling.

Polly wondered where Kolya had gone. Having seen the king he had completed his business in Brighton, she realised dejectedly. He had probably left town for good.

As it happened, Kolya had ridden up to Dean House shortly after Nick left to look for his sister. He wanted to see Polly. He had never seen her angry before, and it had shaken his confidence that she was coming to love him as much as he loved her. Though he had expected her to be vexed with him for concealing his identity, the depth of her resentment puzzled him. It had not seemed a good moment to try to explain his intentions, but surely she must have calmed down by now.

When Mrs. Borden announced that Miss Howard was not at home, he assumed that she refused to see him. She needed more time. He would not press her, but perhaps Lady Sylvia might put in a good word for him.

"I may speak to her ladyship?" he enquired. "For a few minutes only."

He was ushered into Lady Sylvia's sitting room. She greeted him with a worried look in her brown eyes.

"Good evening, Prince. Pray be seated."

"I beg do not call me thus, ma'am. In England am Mr. Volkov. I hoped to see Miss Howard but she is still angry, I think?"

"I fear Polly is convinced that you have been laughing at her all the time she has known you. In her eyes, your friendship was a mockery, a joke."

"Joke! Ah no, was no joke."

"She cannot believe that a genuine friendship is possible between a prince and a family with no claim to distinction."

"Is no joke." Kolya ran his fingers through his hair. "This I will prove to her. Even if she will not see me, I must continue arrangements for exhibition. I will go to

Loxwood to fetch paintings."

"To . . . to Loxwood?" Lady Sylvia faltered, paling.

Kolya wondered at her emotion. "Ned will give me pictures for exhibition," he said confidently. "You wish that I take message? Is more problem with your estate?"

"No. Yes. No." She looked down at her twisting hands, her golden ringlets hiding her face. "I owe Mr. Howard an apology," she blurted out. "I *cannot* write it, I must give it in person. Will you try to bring him back with you? Make some excuse. Tell him Polly needs him, or Nick."

"I will say Polly is unhappy and wishes to see *matyushka* — her mother. Mrs. Howard will not travel without escort of Ned."

Her ladyship brightened. "Oh yes. Tell her I hope she will stay here at Dean House, that everything shall be done to make her comfortable. Surely Ned cannot be so angry with me that he will not bring his mother here."

Kolya hid a smile at her slip of the tongue. The use of Ned's Christian name confirmed the suspicion that more than a desire to apologize lay behind her urgency to see him.

"Ned is not one to bear a grudge," he said.

"Nor is Polly," she assured him eagerly.

"I daresay by the time you return she will have forgotten she was miffed at you."

"I trust you are correct, ma'am." His spirits rose. "If I am lucky she will be planning a new picture and will have no thought for anything else. I ride tonight to Loxwood."

He bowed over her hand, promised to bring Ned back with him, and took his leave.

His borrowed steed was a sweet goer and he an expert horseman. In the moonlit night the miles fled swiftly beneath them. Nonetheless, by the time he reached Loxwood it was far too late for paying social calls. Kolya knew that he would be made welcome at the manor whatever the hour of his arrival, and he could see Ned in the morning. Impatient, he decided to ride past the Howards' house on the off chance that Ned might be sitting up late.

A crack of light showed between the curtains of the office. Kolya dismounted and knocked on the open window.

"Ned," he called softly.

"Who is there?" The curtains were flung back and Ned held up a candle. "Mr. Volkov! Is Polly ill? Or Nick?"

"No, no, my dear fellow. All is well. And what is this return to formality? Are we not friends?" He wanted to be sure of his ground before he revealed his title.

"Will you come in, Kolya?" Ned was slightly flushed. "I'll open the front door. I'm finished with my bookkeeping anyway. You had best stable your horse with Chipper."

They rubbed down the horse in companionable silence, fed and watered him, then went into the house. Ned led the way to the sitting room and poured them each a glass of brandy.

"*Za zdorovye.*" Kolya raised his glass in salute and sipped, feeling a pleasant lethargy steal over him.

"Your health." Ned returned the toast. They chatted about Loxwood for a few minutes, then he topped up the glasses and said, "Don't think you are not welcome, but I suppose you had a reason for your return and for calling at this hour?"

Until that moment Kolya had not been sure how much he was going to tell his beloved's brother. The brandy loosened his tongue, and he plunged straight in. "Polly is very angry with me."

"Oh?" said Ned noncommittally. "Why is that?"

Kolya swallowed a strengthening draught. Unlike vodka, brandy was meant to be sipped, but it went down very smoothly, and he followed it with some more before confessing, "Because she discovered I am a prince."

"A what!" Ned too had recourse to his glass. Being unused to swigging large quantities of spirituous liquors, he choked. His face scarlet, he gasped for air and tears started in his eyes. Kolya dashed to the kitchen and brought back a glass of water. Ned took it gratefully, quenched his burning throat, and demanded, "Did you say just now what I think you said?"

"I am a prince. My father is a prince. My mother is a princess, and my brothers and sisters are princes and princesses. In Russia are many princes." He fortified himself once more, noticing that his companion was sipping again, with caution. Refilling their glasses he went on, "Polly is angry that I did not tell her."

"Don't blame her."

"You too are angry?"

Ned appeared to search his mind, then shook his head. "Don't think so. But I unnerstand why Poll is. Rotten thing to do to a girl."

"Lady Sylvia told me Polly thinks I was mocking her, pretending friendship."

"Fine woman, Lady Sylvia. *Very* fine

woman. Love her," said Ned with drunken earnestness. Kolya recalled that in general he was most abstemious. "Want to marry her," he went on, "take care of her, but she's a lady 'n' I'm jus' a bailiff."

"She wishes to see you. She told me to bring you back with me." With the clarity of detachment Kolya noted that as usual his English improved when he was slightly top heavy — and a fine English idiom that was.

Ned brightened, then sank back into gloom. "No good," he said despondently, shaking his head. "Ever'one'll say 'm a for . . . a for . . . a fortune hunter. 'Sides, all she wants is to offer me a job again. You really a prince?"

"Yes, but a destitute prince. I want to marry your sister, but I cannot support a wife."

"No good." Ned shook his head again, this time finding it difficult to stop. "No money no good, an' anyway a prince can't marry a commoner. An' anyway, Polly don' want to marry anyway . . . anyone. De'cated to art. Husban'll stop her painting. Tol' me so. 'Swhy won't marry Lord Fitz."

"I shall not stop her painting. I wish to encourage her." With some surprise he remembered the purpose of his journey. "There is going to be an exhibition of her work in Brighton. I came to fetch her pictures."

"Goo' fellow, Kolya." A huge yawn overcame him. His eyelids drooped, and Kolya was just in time to rescue his glass from suddenly slack fingers.

Ned was no lightweight. After carrying him up the stairs, dropping him on his bed, and pulling off his boots, Kolya decided against saddling up and riding on to the manor. He removed his own boots, coat, and neckcloth, abstracted a quilt and a pillow from under his snoring friend, and dossed down on the floor.

Prince or no, on the long journey between St Petersburg and Tunbridge Wells he had slept in many worse places.

16

The hired chaise bearing Mrs. Howard and her daughter's pictures, escorted by Ned and Kolya on horseback, reached Brighton early the next evening. As they passed the church on its hill and continued down Church Street, the white domes of the Pavilion blazed in the golden light.

"I am certain that Polly must be painting," Kolya said to Ned. "I wish to look for her. You will continue to Dean House?"

Absorbed in his own thoughts, Ned merely nodded. Kolya trotted south on the New Road wondering just how much his friend remembered of their conversation last night.

Polly was just where he expected to find her. Concentrating on her painting, she did not notice his approach, so he rode on to the vast, domed Royal Stables, left his mount, and walked back to her.

"Kolya!" She looked up with a glad smile in her deep blue eyes. A matching smear of indigo decorated her chin, he noticed with loving amusement. Her smile faded. "I beg your pardon — Your Excellency."

He shook his head, laughing. "First thought is best thought, Polly. Lady Sylvia told you I have gone to fetch your pictures for the exhibition?"

"Yes, and I'm very grateful." She sighed. "How difficult it is to continue resenting your deception when you are so kind!"

"Is much too difficult. You must not try." He tore his gaze from her rueful face, turning to the canvas on her easel where sunset-flushed domes stood out against a darkening sky. "This painting is one of your best, I think. Will be ready in time?"

"Yes, just a few finishing touches." She returned to her work. "I caught it at precisely the right moment yesterday. Oh, Kolya, Nick and I were looking for you yesterday. We saw some most peculiar goings-on down in the Pavilion cellars, but no one would take any notice of what we said."

"In the cellars! Why were you and Nick in the cellars?"

"We followed some men." Continuing to paint, she explained.

"I have a bone to pluck with young Nicholas," he said grimly, when she finished the story.

"Bone to pick. Crow to pluck," said Polly, setting down her paintbrush. "There, that's done."

"Was wrong to take you with him," Kolya persisted.

"I could not let him go alone, and I could not stop him. Anyway, there has been no outcry so it seems they did no harm." She began to pack up her equipment. "Those who refused to believe us were right."

He was not so sure. "Where did you see these men?" he asked, helping her fold the easel. "Where did they enter the Pavilion?"

She pointed towards the southern end of the building. "We first noticed them over there. They went through a door in the southern end, by the kitchens, and . . . Kolya, look! Did you see him?" She clutched his arm with multicoloured fingers.

A furtive figure with a coil of rope slung over his shoulder dashed from one bush to the next. "Yes, I see, and there is another. I must follow."

"It's much earlier than yesterday, there are only two of them, and they have no barrels. Perhaps they are nothing to do with the others."

"They move as you described, to stay hidden." Probably because they did not wish to be seen taking a short cut across the Pavilion grounds — Kolya did not really believe anything was seriously amiss. He rather fancied the smuggled brandy theory; it would be typical of the crazy English, he felt, to have a king who was in league with smugglers.

However, no more than Nick could he resist the possibility of an adventure. "I will follow."

"Then I'm coming too. If it's the same men, then I can show you which way they went. Here, take these." She thrust the easel and her paint box into his hands, picked up her stool and the canvas in its sling, and set out in pursuit.

Kolya caught up with her and made an unsuccessful effort to dissuade her from going with him. Together they hurried between the piles of building materials, then through the bushes, until Polly stopped and pointed out the door by which she and Nick had entered the Pavilion.

The men had disappeared. Probably they had gone innocently about their own business, but in any case Kolya wanted to investigate. He headed for the door, Polly close at his heels.

The cellars were just as she had described them. They left her painting things hidden near the entrance and made their way cautiously towards the far end.

"I don't believe they are here," Polly whispered. "I haven't seen a sign of them. Yesterday we kept catching glimpses. I'll show you the room they went into, though."

The door to the room was ajar when they reached it, outlined by a dim light beyond. Effortful grunts and the sound of heavy objects being moved issued from within. Kolya crept closer, trying to see what was going on without being seen.

The light wavered and went out.

"Hell and damnation," swore a hoarse voice softly. "Didn't you refill the bloody lantern, you fool?"

"I thought there were plenty left." The second man sounded scared.

"We'll have to pinch some oil from one of them lamps. Come on, hurry."

Uncertain footsteps approached the door. Kolya moved backwards, nearly stumbling over Polly who was once again at his heels. Two men came out of the room and made for the nearest unlit lamp.

"Stay here," Kolya hissed over his shoulder and slipped into the room. It was pitch dark but for the faintest of illumination from a distant lamp farther down the cellar.

As he paused to allow his eyes to adjust, that illumination was momentarily cut off and he realised Polly had followed him — and the bobbing light of the lantern was close behind her. He pulled her back against the wall, found her hand, and felt his way around to the far side of the room, cursing himself for letting her come with him.

The brick wall gave way to a dirt-lined alcove. They crouched there, huddling into the corner, as the narrow beam of the dark lantern played over the pile of barrels in the center of the brick floor.

"It'll do," said the hoarse voice. "Give that lantern here."

"I dunno," the other whimpered. "It don't seem like such a good idea, after all."

"Why should his fat majesty revel in luxury he ain't paid for while our children starve," the first man snarled. The lantern moved abruptly, bobbing floorward. "There. Let's get a move on now."

Before Kolya could react, the door slammed shut and the key clicked in the lock.

The lantern was gone but a flickering light provided a brief glimpse of Polly's white face as he sprang up. He knew what he would find as he strode round the stack of barrels.

Towards the stack a lilac flame crawled inexorably, releasing suffocating fumes. He had seen similar fuses used by Russian sappers — a core of compressed gunpowder wrapped in waxed hemp, burning at two feet per minute. Ten feet to the point where it disappeared under the nearest barrel, one of a pyramid he could not hope to move so fast.

Dropping to his knees beside the fuse, he felt in his pocket. "You have knife? Quick."

Polly was at his side, handing him the little penknife she used to sharpen her charcoal sticks. "Can I do anything to help?" Her voice trembled.

"Pull it taut. Will cut more easily." He sawed at the sinister snake with the pitifully frail blade.

Raising the brass lion-head door-knocker, Ned wondered what his reception at Dean House would be. Vaguely he recalled opening his heart to Kolya last night, but just what had been said escaped him. He was ashamed of his overindulgence.

Though he had come to Brighton today to escort his mother, at her insistence, he knew that sooner or later he would have had to see Lady Sylvia again. Her sweet face had haunted his dreams since he stormed away from Westcombe in a passion of hurt and despair. He was ashamed of that, too. In general his temper was as equable as his sister's, and he should have turned down the offer of a position with calm courtesy. But he did not want to be her agent!

One of the maids opened the door. "Oh, sir, her ladyship'll be that glad you're come!" She turned and called down the hall, "Mrs. Borden! Mrs. Borden, 'tis Mr. Howard."

Ned saw the plump housekeeper hurrying towards them, wringing her hands, her face sagging with worry, and his pleasure at his welcome faded. "What is it?" he demanded. "What's wrong?"

"It's Miss Nettie and Miss Winnie, sir, and Master Nick. He's that good about bringing them home for their tea, but they should have been in an hour and more since."

"What is it, Ned?" called Mrs. Howard from the chaise. "Did I hear Nicky's name?"

She was fumbling with the door. Ned hurried back to help her out, paid the coachman and gave him swift orders to unload the luggage and Polly's pictures. By the time he turned back to the front door, Lady Sylvia was standing on the step. He led his mother to her. It did not seem the moment for formal introductions.

"I daresay it is nothing," said her ladyship, her lower lip trembling, "but you know how good Nick has always been about bringing the girls home on time. I beg your pardon, Mrs. Howard, this is a poor welcome. Pray come in."

"Where's my Nicky?" she asked suspiciously, stepping over the threshold.

"He took my daughters for a walk, ma'am, as he does often. He has been very good to them. I'm sure he has simply forgotten the time." Lady Sylvia turned to Ned and held out both hands. "Only I cannot help remembering the threats Mr. Welch uttered when you . . . when I was forced to dismiss him."

Ned took her hands in a comforting clasp but had to release them at once when his mother let out a shriek.

"Nicky! He has been abducted and murdered, I know it!"

"Of course he has not, Mother. Welch was all bluff and bluster."

"Come and sit down, Mrs. Howard." Lady Sylvia regained her composure as the older woman lost hers. "You must be quite tired out after your journey. Ned — Mr. Howard is quite right about Mr. Welch, of course; it was foolish of me to think of him. They are not so very late. Mrs. Borden, tea in my sitting room, if you please."

Ned followed the ladies, his heart overflowing with love as he saw how her ladyship soothed and comforted his mother. As soon as Mrs. Howard was settled on the chaise longue and a maid had been sent for lavender water and hartshorn, he asked quietly, "They are gone up on the downs? I shall go and look for them at once."

The look in her soft brown eyes told him that his reassurance about the dismissed overseer had convinced her no more than it had convinced him. She pressed her lips together, then said in a tolerably steady voice, "Please. I will take care of your mama. Be careful."

He could not resist kissing her hand before he strode from the room, across the terrace and garden, and out through the gate in the wall.

The sun was still well above the horizon, the long July day scarcely waning. As he climbed the slope, Ned's fear that Welch might have abducted the children warred with his happiness in Sylvia's dependence on him. He hallooed as he went, stopping to peer down into every green coomb. They could not have gone far, he thought; the little girls had short legs.

Walking the crests of the hills, he circled

the deep valley where he had strolled with Sylvia so short a time before. Nick had talked of playing hide-and-seek in the bushes down there, and there was the ruined house, though he had promised to stay away from it.

An hour passed during his circuit. Another hour and darkness would be drawing near. Ned hurried down into the valley, shouting his brother's name.

As he pushed through the bushes, he realised that they were the remnant of an abandoned shrubbery — laurels, ilex, and privet — now tied together in an almost impenetrable thicket by ivy and wild clematis. He emerged into a clearing where rose bushes flourished in tangled abandon, a profusion of scented flowers reverting to their single-petalled ancestors after years without pruning. From here the house was clearly visible.

He had not been close to it before. Now he saw that it was indeed a ruin, nothing left of the centre part and the south wing but charred timbers. The north wing was somewhat better preserved, if no more livable. The roof had caved in and the windows of the upper floors gaped glassless, but the westering sun struck shards of light from the ground-floor windows. Purple-pink fireweed grew tall through the gaps in the terrace paving.

If his brother and Sylvia's daughters were not there, Ned had no idea where to look next. He started towards the house.

"Nick!" he called. "Annette! Edwina!" He paused. Was that a shout? "Nicholas?"

"Ned!"

A figure appeared at a first-floor window. Ned broke into a run, flailing at the rose branches that caught his clothes and scratched his face. By the time he reached the house, Nick was emerging from a doorless doorway.

"Lord, Ned, I'm devilish glad to see you." He was filthy, his hands, face, and clothes smeared with black. "Come in, quickly. The girls get frightened if I leave them. That's why I couldn't go for help."

"What's happened? What are you doing here?" Ned followed his brother into the house.

"Careful on these stairs, they're shaky. We were playing hide-and-seek, and Winnie decided the best hiding places must be in here. I think she just plain forgot she wasn't supposed to go near the house. She's only little." He stopped at the top of the creaking stairs and barred the way. "This is where it gets difficult."

"Where are they?"

"Just around the corner. Winnie went into a room and shut the door, and it's stuck. I can't budge it an inch. The trouble is, the floor's in rotten shape. Annette," he called, "we're coming."

Ned saw that the landing floor was burned through in places, revealing the joists. As Nick stepped cautiously onto it, a piece of wood fell clattering to the floor below.

"I suppose Winnie is so light she crossed easily," Ned observed.

"Yes, and Annette, too. She's game as a pebble, such a sensible creature. She's sitting outside the door talking to Winnie. You have to go around by the wall — it's stronger there — and watch that you place your feet directly above a joist. If you look at the holes you can see where they run."

Pressing close to the scorched plaster, Ned followed Nick. Fortunately the floor of the passage beyond the landing was in much better shape, the boards charred but solid. Above, the ceiling was gone, only a crisscrossed litter of timbers separating the intruders from the twilight sky.

Annette was sitting on the floor, hugging her knees, her face pale in the gloom. Her tremulous smile, so like her mother's, made

Ned's heart turn over.

"We shall soon have your sister safe, love," he said, crouching to put his arm about her thin shoulders with a gentle squeeze. "The best place for you will be under a door lintel, I think. Come and stand over here in this doorway and don't stir, while Nick and I have a go at that door. Nick, do you know what the floor is like in the room?"

"Winnie says it's solid."

Ned glanced up at the heavy beams lying across the passage and tried not to think what would happen if their efforts dislodged them. Their settling weight must have distorted the walls, jamming the door. He went over to the door, put his mouth close to it and said, "Winnie, you must go over to the farthest corner. Stay away from the window but keep close against the wall. We'll have you out of there right away."

He put his shoulder to the door and heaved. Nothing happened.

"Told you it's stuck," Nick said. "We'll have to charge it. I thought of using a battering ram, but there isn't enough clearance."

The passage was about four feet wide. Together the brothers threw themselves across it, hitting the door shoulder-first. It burst open with a crash. Ned, on the latch side, hurtled into the room and sprawled full length. He pushed himself up, and sank back with a groan. His shoulder was on fire, shooting arrows of agony up his neck and down into his ribcage.

Two small feet shod in kid half-boots appeared before his eyes. "Did you hurt yourself, sir?" enquired Winnie in dismay.

The difficult return around the landing was excruciating, and the walk back to Dean House seemed endless. Winnie, tired but otherwise undamaged in body and spirit, rode on Nick's shoulders. Ned offered Annette his good hand, which she took after asking with touching solicitude if he was sure it would not make the pain worse. He found that it was bearable as long as he kept up a slow, steady pace, but the slightest independent movement of his arm, hidden beneath his coat in its makeshift sling, brought torture. Not wanting to upset the children, he managed to hold back his groans.

Nick lifted Winnie down to go through the door in the garden wall. The two girls dashed ahead through the deep dusk towards the welcoming light in the uncurtained windows of Lady Sylvia's sitting room. When Ned and Nick reached the

French doors, they were in their mother's arms, babbling the tale of their adventure, interrupting each other and both talking at once.

Over their heads, Lady Sylvia saw Ned step into the room. She set her daughters aside and came swiftly to him, her eyes alight with joy and gratitude.

She put her arms around his neck. He fainted.

The first voice to penetrate Ned's consciousness was his mother's, but the gentle hands that bathed his forehead with lavender water were Sylvia's. He was about to open his eyes when soft lips touched his cheek, followed by a teardrop, and a soft voice murmured, "Oh, my brave dear."

Unfortunately, the next voice to make itself heard was Nick's. "Where's Polly?"

The only answer was a shocked silence. Ned opened his eyes at last. It was pitch dark now — and Polly *always* came home by nightfall.

17

A spark burned Polly's hand as the last strand parted. She let go. Kolya picked up the remaining foot of the fuse and flung it into a corner. For half a minute they watched it fizzle and sputter, then it went out. Darkness and silence closed in.

She reached out towards him, and suddenly she was in his arms. He held her close. The rough brick beneath her knees vanished and she was conscious only of his warm breath on her cheek, the long leanness of him pressed against her.

"Polly," he murmured, "Polly," and his voice shook.

For a moment which seemed endless but was all too short, she clung to him. Then he released her and helped her up.

"The door is this way, I think," he said matter-of-factly.

"They locked it. I heard them."

"I too, but I must try." Holding her hand, he moved cautiously forward. "Come, I do not want to lose you."

Polly stretched her other hand ahead of her. The absolute absence of light was blacker than she had ever imagined, yet she peered into it, straining her eyes to see the invisible. The only sound was the shuffle of their feet, then Kolya stopped.

"Here is the wall. The door must be near."

She took another step and her fingertips hit wood. "It's here." Waving her hand, she found the handle, turned it. "And it's locked."

"Then here we will stay until we are found. Best we sit down and make as comfortable as we can."

"Nick will guess where we are."

"Of course. Do not say my fearless one is afraid?" he teased, pulling her down to sit against the wall, his arm around her waist.

Her hat was in the way, so she pulled it off. "No, but I would be if you were not here. And I would have been before, if there had been time. They were trying to blow up the king!"

"His Majesty's suite is just above us — his bathroom or his dressing room. At this moment he is probably dressing for the dinner. Was well planned."

"It was very wicked of them, but I cannot help sympathizing a little. I recognized one of the men yesterday. His business was ruined by the construction. Do you think I ought to give him away?"

"Give him away?"

"Inform against him. Tell that I saw him. No, I cannot! He would probably be hanged. But suppose they try again?"

"I doubt they will, especially if I speak to this man so that he knows he is discovered."

"And if I tell you who he is, you will not lay information against him?"

She heard the grin in his voice. "I am not a friend of the authorities. You know why I was exiled from Russia — for rescuing a prisoner from my own emperor."

"Will you tell me about it? Lady John said a little, but I should like to hear the whole story."

Kolya's description of Lord John disguised as an imperial footman made her laugh, and the horrors of the dungeons of the Peter Paul fortress made their own cellar seem almost cosy in comparison. Not quite. By the time his tale was finished, the chill was seeping through her thin summer gown and she began to shiver.

"You are cold!" He moved away from her, withdrawing the one patch of warmth. "You must put on my coat."

"Then you will be cold."

"I have the leather riding breeches. Besides, it is the privilege of a gentleman to freeze so that a lady will not. Now, put your arm here."

In the process of helping her into his coat in the pitch darkness, his hands brushed against her body, feathered across her breasts, settled for a moment on the back of her neck. She was glowing with heat long before he fastened the buttons and put his arm back around her waist.

Of its own accord her head came to rest against his shoulder. In the ringing silence she felt the tension in him, heard his quickened breathing.

If he wanted her, she would give herself to him without a second thought. She knew it without a doubt. How wrong she had been to think her principles were strong enough to withstand her attraction to Kolya! Marriage was not for her, but she would take whatever he offered.

Her hand crept to his chest. It came to rest on the icon he always wore about his neck, under his shirt. He put his own hand over hers, pressed it, sighed, and began to talk about his mother and his sisters.

Gradually she relaxed, and even dozed. When she woke to feel his cheek resting against the top of her head, she kept quite still so as not to disturb him and soon drifted off to sleep again. Then they both woke at the same time and walked cautiously around the edge of the room, Kolya trailing his fingers against the wall, to restore their circulation before settling again.

"It feels as if we have been here for days," Polly said as they set out on their third tour of the room. "How long do you think it will take Nick to persuade someone to come and look for us?"

"Ned will be with him," Kolya reminded her, "and Ned looks too respectable to be ignored."

"Unlike me in my painting smock," she had to admit. "If only it weren't so dark. I'm beginning to imagine I see things. Things like huge, crusty loaves of bread, fresh from the oven, and yellow rounds of cheese, and dishes of strawberries and cream. You know, I think my next painting will be a still life of food."

Kolya laughed. "Excellent idea. I will buy. Ah, we are halfway around. Here is the hole in the wall."

"The niche where we hid? I wonder what it's doing there. Do you suppose it could be part of their plot — to weaken the walls so they crumble more easily?"

"I believe is beginning of a tunnel. Mr.

Nash is to build an underground passage for the king, so that he can go to the stables privately."

"I heard that he is too heavy to ride. There was an article in the *Times*, it must have been five years ago, about his difficulty in mounting. Ned told me about it. They had to build a special contraption."

"What is contraption?"

"This one was a slope, about two feet high, I think, with a platform at the top. They would push Prinny up on a chair with rollers, then the platform was raised by some sort of screw mechanism until it was high enough for a horse to pass under it. Then Prinny was lowered onto the horse and off he went."

Kolya was shouting with laughter when the door opened. Polly screwed her eyes shut against a flood of light as half a dozen people poured into the room. When she opened them Ned was standing in front of her, dear, respectable Ned with his arm in a sling, smears of what looked very like soot all over his clothes, and a huge grin on his scratched face.

"What's the joke?" he asked, then fended off her attempted hug with his good arm. "No, don't touch me, I've done something frightful to my shoulder. You, on the other hand, look to be in fine fettle."

Nick left the other four men, one a footman and two in military uniform, who were more interested in the barrels of gunpowder than the pair they had rescued.

"What happened?" he demanded. "Jupiter, I knew there was something smoky going on."

Kolya explained, "Was plot to explode king."

After their discussion of His Majesty's excessive girth, Polly suspected that his choice of words was deliberate. His face was innocent, but there was a gleam in his *eye*. Luckily the soldier who now turned towards them didn't notice.

"We'll need to know everything you saw and heard, ma'am, sir," he said grimly.

Suddenly Polly was exhausted. "I want to go home!" she wailed. Ned, looking equally tired, put his good arm around her.

"Just a few questions," said the officer in a harassed voice. "Come upstairs and we'll make you comfortable, ma'am." He ordered the other soldier to stand guard, then led the way out of the cellars.

They emerged in a part of the Pavilion Polly had not visited. She caught sight of a clock — it was past three in the morning. The officer ushered them, Ned and Nick too, into a small room with a large desk and stacks of papers everywhere.

"Sit down, I shall be with you in a moment," he said.

He was turning to leave when Nick said loudly, "Some tea for my sister, sir!"

"Bless you," said Polly, sinking onto one of the hard chairs as the soldier nodded and shut the door behind him. They heard him issuing commands in the corridor.

He returned in a few minutes with two other men. One he introduced as the king's equerry and the second appeared to be a secretary, as he wrote down everything Kolya and Polly said. They denied adamantly that they had any idea who had planted the gunpowder, and, following Kolya's lead, Polly did not mention the plotters' motive. Nick was equally reticent when the officer turned to him for confirmation of his sister's story.

There was not a great deal to tell. They were finished by the time a footman brought in tea, wine, and sandwiches. Ned and Nick had also missed their dinner so the interrogation turned into an impromptu picnic, though Polly was too tired to do more than nibble.

She was about once more to proclaim her desire to go home, when another footman entered and spoke to the equerry.

With a look of annoyance, that gentleman announced, "His Majesty wishes to thank Miss Howard and . . . ah . . . Prince Nikolai in person."

"But it's past three o'clock," Polly protested.

"His Majesty is . . . ah . . . celebrating."

The officer who had been drumming his fingers impatiently on the desk, broke in. "The news came this evening that the Privy Council has denied Queen Caroline's request to be crowned."

The equerry frowned at him as if he thought it none of their business just what the king was celebrating. He turned back to Polly. "I . . . ahem . . . might I suggest, ma'am, that you return His . . . ah . . . Excellency's coat?"

She had quite forgotten that she was wearing Kolya's coat. Clumsy with fatigue, she struggled with the buttons. He was beside her in an instant, gently pushing her fingers aside and undoing them. As he helped her take off the coat, a gasp of dismay from the equerry reminded her that under it was her painting smock. However, he had not the nerve to ask a lady to disrobe further and she was far too tired to bother. Dishevelled and dirty as they were, she and

Kolya followed him across a corridor and into a long, elegantly furnished room.

Compared to the greater part of the Pavilion, the king's library was modestly decorated. Between inset bookshelves, the wall panels were light green with white floral patterns, and the ceiling was pale blue with fluffy white clouds. There was not a dragon in sight.

By the white marble fireplace, where a fire blazed despite the warmth of the night, a lady sat with her back to them. Opposite her a vast gentleman in a crimson dressing gown with gold tasselled cord was raising his glass in a toast. His face matched his robe. As the equerry led them closer, Polly saw that the table with bottles and glasses had seen a great deal more use than the chess set on its stand between the pair. Only a single pawn had been moved.

"Miss Howard and Prince Nikolai Volkov, sir."

Kolya bowed and Polly curtsied to the floor. As she rose, she saw that the woman was Lady Conyngham.

"Well, Prince," said the king jovially, "we hear you have saved us from a second Guy Fawkes."

From the corner of her eye, Polly noted that Kolya looked blank. She would have to explain Guy Fawkes to him. He bowed again and said, "Was my pleasure, sir."

"I'll wager it was a pleasure, with so fair a companion. So this is your artistic protégée?" He regarded her smock with an amused twinkle. "I have your cherry tree in bloom, Miss Howard, a delightful piece."

"Thank you, sir," Polly murmured, blushing and bobbing another curtsy. His Majesty might be near as big around as an elephant but he had retained the genial charm of his youth.

"It was you, I hear, ma'am, who first suspected this gunpowder plot. We are deeply indebted to you, and you shall both be properly rewarded. But you are sorely fatigued. We must not keep you longer from your rest."

"My dear sir," put in Lady Conyngham, patting his fat hand, "surely you wish to assure the happy couple of your blessing on their marriage."

"Marriage?" said His Majesty, frowning as if the word was an obscenity. Kolya looked not much better pleased.

"Prince Nikolai and Miss Howard have spent the greater part of the night alone together," her ladyship pointed out. "Her reputation will be ruined if they are not wed at once."

"No!" cried Polly. "I beg you, sir, do not force us to wed. I am an artist and dedicated to my work. It is my intention to remain single."

"I'll not be party to pushing any man into marriage," declared the king roundly, "nor any woman neither. It is by no means a desirable estate, my dear Lady Conyngham. Nor is our realm so overrun with fine artists that it can afford to lose any to the whims of a husband. If none know of this night's doings, Miss Howard's reputation will not suffer, and any who babble of it shall incur our extreme displeasure." He glared at the equerry.

"I shall see that it is kept quiet, sir," said that unoffending gentleman, and hurried Polly and Kolya from the room.

Polly was too tired and bewildered to take in the events of the next few minutes. The equerry muttered that she was lucky to have found His Majesty in an obliging humour. The officer told them not to leave Brighton for the next few days. Kolya disappeared. She was reunited with Ned and Nick, and a carriage was provided to return them to Dean House through streets shiny with rain.

Mama and Lady Sylvia greeted her with tears of relief, but dazed as she was she could not help noticing that a greater share of Sylvia's care was lavished on Ned. It was good to have Mama there, helping her undress, tutting over her smock, putting her nightgown over her head, and tucking her up in bed as if she were a little child again.

At last she was alone. All she could think of was that she had had a chance to marry Kolya and had rejected it. She loved him and wanted him, but she could not bear that he should be forced to wed her.

18

None the worse for wear, Nick thudded into Ned's chamber at noon, set a steaming pitcher on the washstand, and flung back the curtains to reveal the first wet day in months.

"I've come to lend a hand," he announced. "How are you feeling?"

"In prime twig." Despite the throbbing ache in his shoulder and the dismal weather outside, Ned was filled with joyful anticipation.

"You're to breakfast in bed. Mother's orders."

As Nick helped him wash his face and hands and comb his hair, Ned tried to subdue his hopes. Lady Sylvia had been grateful for his rescue of Winnie and solicitous of the injury received in her service, but he must certainly have imagined anything more. A gently bred, bashful young widow could not have kissed his cheek, let alone called him her dear.

All his tender thoughts vanished when

Nick approached him with shaving brush and razor.

"Not on your life!"

"I shaved the fellows I fagged for at Winchester," said Nick, injured. "I'll be shaving myself soon." He dabbed hopefully at his upper lip.

"Send for a barber. He'll be here by the time I'm ready to dress."

"All right, but you're going to regret it." Grinning mischievously, he opened the door, stepped outside, and said, "He's decent, sort of. I'll take that teapot, it's heavy."

Bearing a tray, Lady Sylvia glided into the room, her eyes lowered, a faint blush tingeing her cheeks with rose. Ned felt his stubbled chin and silently cursed his brother for not warning him. Still grinning, Nick set the teapot on a small table, took the tray from her ladyship and set it on Ned's lap, and moved a straight chair to the bedside.

"Pray be seated, ma'am," he requested with a sweeping bow, then headed for the door, which he closed firmly behind him.

Ned's gaze was on her face, but he had a distinct impression that his wretched younger brother had glanced back and winked on his way out of the room.

"I'll pour you some tea," said Sylvia hurriedly, taking the cup and saucer from the tray. At the table, her back to him, she added, "I . . . I thought you might need some help eating."

"I do," he said softly, though he hadn't looked to see what was on his plate.

Still not meeting his eyes, she brought the cup of tea and set it on his tray. She sat down in the chair Nick had placed for her and leaned forward to cut up the cold sirloin. The tray wobbled.

"You can't do it from there. Come and sit here." Ned patted the side of the bed.

Fiery faced she obeyed, but he caught her hand before she could return to knife and fork.

"I'm not really hungry. Sylvia, tell me if I am presuming — I can't help myself. Our stations are so very unequal, but I have never met another woman like you. I love you, and I want to take care of you. Will you be my wife?"

At last she met his urgent gaze and he read love and need glowing in her brown eyes. Modest, bashful Lady Sylvia leaned forward and kissed him full on the mouth.

The tray tilted, the tea spilled, and a steady drip soaked the sheets. Neither Sylvia nor Ned noticed.

Some time later, a soft but determined
tapping on the door recalled them to the
world. Sylvia jumped up, snatched up her
cap and sped to the mirror on the dresser to
smooth her hair.

"Who is there?" Ned called.

"It's just us, sir." Winnie tugged Annette
into the room. "Have you finished your
breakfast? Nick said you're going to marry
Mama." She marched to the bedside and
confronted him. "What we want to know is,
will you please be our papa, too?"

"If you think I shall suit, I shall be delighted," he said gravely.

"Oh yes, you will suit. We like you, don't
we, Annette?"

Her solemn sister nodded.

"Then come and give me a kiss, girls, to
seal the bargain." Beaming, Winnie started
to scramble onto the bed, then stopped with
a gasp. "You've spilled your tea," she whispered. "Mama will be cross."

"Then don't let's tell her," he whispered
back. Over the two small, golden heads, he
saw his beloved examining a wet patch on
her gown in dismay. Catching her eye, he
blew her a kiss. She returned it with a blush
as she hurried off to change out of the in-
criminating garment.

Ned leaned back against his pillows with a sigh of contentment and allowed his two new daughters to feed him his breakfast.

When Nick came to help him dress, he was too happy to issue a stern reprimand at the premature disclosure to Winnie and Annette, though he did grumble.

Nick grinned. "I reckoned it would give you a shove in the right direction if you hadn't yet got down to business."

"I trust you said nothing to Mother and Polly!"

"Do you take me for a complete buffle-head? I even swore the girls to secrecy," he said virtuously. "Besides, Polly's still a-bed. Mother says she's to stay there all day to recover from her ordeal."

"Poor Poll. I'll break the news to Mother and then I'll go and see her."

The barber came to shave him, then Ned went downstairs. Mrs. Howard was *aux anges* when she heard of his betrothal.

"An earl's daughter!" she marvelled. "And such a dear girl. Why, she could not have been kinder last night, when we were so worried, if I had been her own mother." She carried on in this vein for some time, then changed course. "Ned, what is this I hear about Mr. Volkov turning out to be a prince? If he has been trifling with our

Polly's affections, you must call him to account."

"It's true he is a prince, Mother, but he is still penniless."

"Oh dear, what a dreadful coil! They were locked in together all night. What will people say?"

"We must hope they will say that the king was saved from a horrid fate and forget the manner of his rescue. Have you talked to Polly about it?"

"I tried, but all she will say is that the prince behaved with perfect propriety and that she wants to go home. But I cannot go home now, indeed I cannot, or people will think I am snubbing dear Sylvia."

Ned soothed her and went up to see Polly in her green-and-white chamber. She was sitting up in bed, looking perfectly healthy and perfectly miserable. For want of any better subject, she was sketching the candlestick and pile of books on her bedside table.

Seeing his sling, she said, "Is your shoulder still painful? Poor Ned."

"I don't need sympathy." He could not help beaming with joy as he perched on the edge of her bed. "Sylvia has consented to marry me."

"My dear, I'm delighted!" Her pleasure was unfeigned, but he noticed a wistful look in her eyes. "You could not have chosen better, and I know you will make her happy."

"I mean to, I promise you. I wish I knew a way to do the same for you. I fear you have set your heart on the unattainable."

Her lips quivered but she spoke with tolerable composure. "I want to go home. I know you will not wish to leave Sylvia so soon, but surely Mama can go with me."

He explained their mother's fear of appearing to slight his betrothed. "Besides, if you both leave I cannot stay in the house, and Sylvia needs my support. We must inform her family, and she dreads their reaction."

"Yet she's willing to face it for your sake. You have won a true treasure. Very well, I'll stay, but please, Ned, I cannot see *him!*"

"Of course you need not." Ned's suspicions were aroused. Despite what she had told Mrs. Howard, was it possible Kolya had made improper advances? "Do you want to tell me why? You're the most independent of sisters, but I'm still responsible for you. I hope you know you can always count on me."

"I know." She laid down her sketch book and reached for his good hand. "You need not feel obliged to defend me, for he was perfectly gentlemanly. But pray do not press me, I don't care to speak of it."

At that moment the maid knocked and came in. "Beg pardon for interrupting, miss, but His Highness has called and he's asking to see you."

Polly clutched Ned's hand.

"Thank you, Jill," he said, "I will come down. My sister is not receiving callers today." He kissed Polly's cheek and followed the maid out of the room. "Are my mother and Lady Sylvia with Mr. Volkov? Prince Nikolai, I mean."

"He did say to tell as Mr. Volkov was calling, sir. No, my lady and Mrs. Howard are writing letters in the sitting room. The gentleman's in the drawing room."

The gentleman was pacing the length of the drawing room, back and forth like a caged wolf, when Ned went in. He turned eagerly at the sound of the door closing.

"How are . . ." His voice died away in disappointment when he saw who had entered. "How are you, Ned? The shoulder is painful still?"

"Yes, but I care nothing for it. Lady Sylvia has done me the honour of consenting to be my wife."

Unsurprised, Kolya strode forward and gripped Ned's good hand. "My dear fellow, *pozdravlayu vas*. I congratulate most heartily."

"You will not mention it to anyone. It's not yet been announced."

"My lip is sealed." He cast about for a polite way to change the subject. Impatience won. "Polly is coming?"

Ned's joyful expression turned to embarrassment. "She . . . er . . . my mother has advised her to keep to her chamber today."

"She is not well?" Kolya asked anxiously. "In the cellar was cold."

"Nothing to worry about, she's just tired."

Ned looked uncomfortable and would not meet his eye. Kolya's eagerness to assure Polly that he would never do anything to thwart her career began to fade. He had not been pleased, last night, when Lady Conyngham had attempted to force Polly to wed him. That was not how he wanted her to come to him. Nonetheless, he had thought that he had only to assure her of his commitment to supporting her work for her to withdraw her objection.

He had high hopes that the king's reward would be sufficiently generous to allow him to take a wife. After all, the tsar often rewarded his favourites with land and serfs. Ready to ask for her hand in exchange for the heart she had long possessed, he was now forced to face the possibility that her outcry in the king's library was a mere excuse.

Her protest that she was a dedicated artist had simply been the denial that first came to mind. If Ned's discomfort now meant anything, it meant that she really didn't want to marry him.

"Ponimayu," he said, the English words washed from him by a wave of coldness more chilling than the bitterest St Petersburg winter because it began in his heart. "I understand. Please convey best wishes for swift recovery." He recalled the other reason for his visit — how unimportant it seemed now! But he would not let her down. "I must take to Mr. Lay the pictures we brought from Loxwood. Is necessary to frame before can be hung."

"Of course." Ned was only too anxious to be of service. "I believe the crates were carried into the coach house. I'll take you there."

Old Dick helped them load the boxes into Kolya's borrowed carriage. His Russian soul filled with gloom, he drove towards the Steyne.

In his back room, Mr. Lay pulled the paintings from the crates one at a time with squeaks of delight. "Splendid. Oh, first rate. Simply bang-up, my dear sir. Or should I say, Your Highness."

"No, you should not," said Kolya, annoyed to find that word of his title had apparently spread throughout the town. Despite his misery, he could not forebear teasing. "Correct address is *'prevoskhoditelstvo.'*"

"I beg pardon, I'm sure, presoveeto." The printseller grimaced as he attempted to twist his tongue around the Russian word.

"Please — it translates as excellency, but here I am plain Mr. Volkov."

"Yes, sir, thank you, sir." He breathed a sigh of relief. "Well, Mr. Volkov, I'm sure the exhibition's going to be a grand success. The lady can expect to sell most all of these, I'd say. I daresay, though, that some are not for sale. If you'd just be so good as to point out to me which belong to other people and which Miss Howard wishes to keep, I'll be sure to mark 'em."

Kolya gazed around at the pictures leaning against the walls. "These have been lent by Lady Sylvia Ellingham," he said, pointing at the child on the Pantiles and a portrait of Winnie and Annette on the swing. "This panorama of Brighton — you sold it, I think."

"Aye, and right glad Dr. Ogilvy is to have it hung in a Royal Exhibition, I can tell you."

"As for the others," he shrugged, and suddenly his spirits rose, "I cannot tell. Must ask Miss Howard." There was his excuse to see her again!

As he returned the carriage to its owner, Kolya's unquenchable optimism revived. He remembered Polly's reaction to his touch, unmistakable even in the pitch dark. If her hand had not alighted on his icon, reminding him of his mother, there was no knowing how far he might have gone. Almost he wished he had taken advantage of that warm, soft, compliant body, had seduced her on the spot — that would have settled her doubts.

But perhaps his fearless Polly was afraid of succumbing to her own feelings. Perhaps, though it seemed impossible to him, she was unsure of his intentions. He had told Ned he wanted to marry her, but Ned had been drunk and in any case would probably not have informed his sister.

Kolya looked back over their relationship. To him it had been a straightforward process of falling in love. To Polly had come shock after shock. In a few short weeks the labourer she had met in the street had become first a gentleman and then a nobleman. It might be better, he thought, to start again from the beginning.

He would woo her slowly and gently until she was unable to hide from herself any longer that she loved him.

After returning the carriage, Kolya walked to the Pavilion. The talk was all of yesterday's decision by the Privy Council to deny the queen her crown. Already the king had set the date of his coronation, the nineteenth of July. As he had spent months planning it, little remained to be done and he would not leave for London until next Monday.

Next Monday, Kolya realised, was the ninth, the day Polly's exhibition opened. He went to find Lady Conyngham to try to persuade her not to set out until she had called at Mr. Lay's shop.

"But of course, dear Prince," she gushed. "I assure you, His Majesty intends to make a detour to visit Miss Howard's exhibition on his way out of Brighton. He is mindful of how much he owes the two of you."

"King himself will come? *Chudesno!* I thank you from the heart, my lady."

"I trust you mean well by that young woman," she chided, diamonds flashing as she shook her plump finger at him. "I daresay a certain amount of eccentricity is permissible in an artist, but God grants no licence to disobey the rules of morality."

Kolya managed to hide his disgust from the pious "vice-queen." "Miss Howard's virtue is safe, ma'am."

"I am glad to hear it. His Majesty is still pondering how best to reward you, and I should not like to think that he was encouraging impropriety."

How dare Lady Conyngham cast aspersions on his Polly's virtue! Though the general opinion was that King George's age, girth, and state of health made it unlikely that the woman was actually his mistress, their relationship was far from innocent. She might read sermons with His Majesty in public, but the pair was not infrequently closeted together in private. Nor was shared piety sufficient to explain the jewels he lavished on her.

Until now, Kolya had regarded her hypocrisy and avarice with the amused tolerance he felt towards most human foibles. He must continue to "turn her up sweet," in the splendid English idiom, for Polly's success might depend on her bringing the king to the exhibition. Her favour or disfavour could also influence the munificence of their rewards.

Not for nothing had Kolya been a courtier as well as a soldier for the past decade. With a few flattering words and expressions of gratitude, he left Lady Conyngham very much in charity with him.

The next morning he went again to Dean House. Mrs. Borden reported that Miss Polly had gone to paint on the downs, Mr. Howard and Master Nick were out, and Lady Sylvia and Mrs. Howard were in the schoolroom, giving Miss Nettie and Miss Winnie their lessons.

Miss *Nettie* and Miss Winnie their lessons.

Regretfully, Kolya decided not to go after Polly. The housekeeper sent a maid to enquire whether her ladyship could receive him, and he was invited to go up to the schoolroom.

As he walked through the door, Winnie jumped down from her chair and ran to hang on his arm. "Mr. Howard's going to be our papa," she informed him excitedly. "Mine and Nettie's."

He congratulated her and her sister, wished Lady Sylvia happy, and agreed with Mrs. Howard on her good fortune in acquiring so delightful a daughter.

"I hoped to see your other daughter,

ma'am," he went on, and explained that Mr. Lay needed Polly's decision about which pictures were for sale and at what price. "As soon as possible," he added. He intended to haunt Mr. Lay's shop until he came face to face with her, quite by accident of course, and he wanted to see her soon.

"Oh dear, she is gone out painting. I shall have to send Nick to fetch her."

"I understand Nick is not at home."

"He will be back. If there is one thing certain in this world," said his mother resignedly, "it's that Nick will come home for luncheon."

19

"But that is one of the pictures the king bought," said Polly, spotting the cherry blossom.

"Indeed it is, Miss Howard." The plump printseller rubbed his hands together, beaming. "His Majesty graciously sent it over with a request that it be hung prominently with his name as the owner."

"How very obliging," whispered Mrs. Howard, awed.

"Pray do the same with mine," Sylvia requested. "Make sure it is plain that they belong to Lady Sylvia Ellingham."

"Certainly, my lady." A bell tinkled in the other room as the street door opened. "Excuse me, ladies, a customer." He bustled out.

Polly continued to look through the canvases, feeling overwhelmed. To be sure the king was obliging, but how much more so was Kolya. None of this would have happened if he had not made it his business to bring it about. Surely such kindness must

indicate a warmer feeling than mere friendship? But no, she remembered that even
Ned had remarked on his willingness to
help a fallen child or an old woman with a
heavy basket. And she remembered the look
of dismay on his face when Lady
Conyngham had said they must marry.

With a start, she realised that that was *his*
voice in the next room. What was she going
to say if he should come through and speak
to her? She strained to hear his words but
only the Russian intonation was plain.

Bending her head, she concentrated on
the pictures, setting aside those she wanted
to keep. There was Kolya's portrait. It
would be hen-witted not to sell that, to have
it always near her, reminding her of his
laughing eyes. Yet she could not bear to part
with it. She picked it up, and saw the tag —
not for sale.

Her mother and Lady Sylvia watched in
astonishment as she rushed into the front
room.

"Why is this already marked?" she demanded, doing her best to keep her gaze on
Mr. Lay and away from Kolya.

It was he who answered, though. "You
gave to me. I wish to keep."

She had to look at him, but she refused to
tell him she wanted it herself. "Why?" she

290

asked. Those slanting hazel eyes were grave, giving her a peculiar feeling that he was trying to see into her mind.

"To remind me of the so pleasant days at Loxwood, Miss Howard. When I look at it, I see the artist."

Oh, but his eyes were laughing now! Probably he was recalling her forgetfulness of time and place, she thought in indignation, and picturing her in her smock with paint on her nose. It was maddening when this afternoon, for once, she was perfectly respectably dressed, in a new gown of midnight blue cambric adorned with amber satin ribbons. She even had a matching spencer of blue and amber striped soie de Londres and a Leghorn hat with matching bows and roses. She certainly hoped he didn't suppose she was wearing them on the off chance of meeting him.

"I did give it to you," she acknowledged reluctantly.

"I wish to commission another portrait, for my mother. You will paint?"

A refusal hovered on her lips. It would be too painful to spend so much time with him. Then she thought of his mother, thousands of miles away, never to see her son again. For all she was a princess, she was also Kolya's — *matyushka,* was that the word?

How she must miss him! A portrait might ease the aching loss a little.

"Very well."

His face lit, and for a moment Polly forgot her feelings and saw with an artist's eye the features she had longed to paint again. She looked down at the portrait in her hands, back at its subject. Perhaps three-quarter profile this time? She reached out and took his chin between finger and thumb. "Turn a little to the left, if you please. That's it. Where's my sketch book?"

He laughed. Blushing furiously, she muttered, "Come tomorrow morning," and fled back to the exhibition room.

Perhaps the confusion she displayed at his teasing laughter troubled him, for when he came the next day he was solemn. He treated her as he did Lady Sylvia, with gentle courtesy and consideration, as if she were no more than an acquaintance. It should have pleased her, since she had determined to be utterly businesslike about the portrait, but instead it left her forlorn.

He must be relieved at her rejection of Lady Conyngham's insistence on marriage, she thought. His mantle of aloofness was intended to remind her of the distance between them. She was afraid that her stupid embarrassment in the print shop had revealed to him at least a hint of her feelings.

She strove to conceal her love, to see his face as nothing but a collection of planes and angles, highlights and shadows. Her sketches came out wooden.

That night, in the privacy of her chamber, she tore them all to shreds. Taking a prepared canvas, she drew him from memory, letting love inform every pencil stroke. Tomorrow she would paint for as many hours as he would pose, and Sunday, too, if necessary, losing herself in her work. On Monday, after the opening day of the exhibition, she would give him his portrait and then go home to Loxwood. Soon the whole family would be moving to Westcombe with Ned and Sylvia, and she need never see Kolya's beloved, tormenting face again.

Good resolutions were all very well, but what was Polly to do when the wretched man turned up with a huge bouquet of roses? Pink, yellow, white, deep crimson, they perfumed the entire house.

"I stole from the Pavilion garden," he confessed with his impish grin, his eyes alight with mischief.

"I suppose the head gardener is one of your bosom bows," she responded tartly, burying her face in the sweet-scented petals.

He had even wrapped the stems in a length of cloth to protect her hands from the thorns.

Roses or no roses, the portrait was finished by Sunday evening. Polly stood it on the mantel in her chamber and lay in bed gazing at it. In the uncertain light of her single bedside candle his expression was haughtily aristocratic, the compensating humour imperceptible. She had decided his mother would prefer a formal depiction, in the well-cut coat and starched neckcloth of a gentleman, the icon clearly visible in his hand. Technically it was better than the first portrait, but Polly infinitely preferred the merry wanderer of the original to this unapproachable nobleman.

She shook her head at her own fancy: unapproachable was an adjective which no one could honestly apply to Kolya, not even the king's gardener. That was what made it so difficult to know how to respond to his friendly overtures.

It was late when she at last fell asleep, and she did not wake the next morning until Lady Sylvia brought her a cup of tea.

"It's ten o'clock," she said, drawing back the ivy-leaf curtains to admit a flood of sunshine, "and your exhibition opens at noon, so we thought you ought to rise soon. You must be horridly nervous."

"Nervous? Heavens no." Polly sat up and reached for the tea, eager to be up and about. "I've dreamed of my own exhibition for years and at last it's come true. I'm not nervous, I'm in *raptures*. You look happy, too. More so than usual, I mean."

"I received a letter from my father this morning. I dreaded that he would storm and rant at me and try to prevent my marrying your brother, but he says he has washed his hands of me." Her delicate features suffused with joy, Sylvia took a paper from her pocket and opened it. "He says I always was a stubborn chit, and as I failed to produce an Ellingham heir my determination to marry a commoner comes as no surprise and is a matter of complete indifference to him. Is it not splendid?"

"Splendid," Polly agreed, laughing. "After all, you washed your hands of him long since. Now if you will please ring for Jill, I shall be dressed in a trice."

"Yes, do hurry down." Sylvia pulled the bell cord. "We are all ready to go with you, even Nick. Oh, I nearly forgot to tell you, there is a letter for you below with the king's seal."

"The king's seal?" Polly jumped out of bed as the maid came in with hot water.

"Why did you not bring it up? Jill, my blue gown, quickly."

"Nick said it would speed you up if you knew it was waiting for you. I see he was right!"

Not half an hour later, Polly in her new blue cambric sped into the sitting room. With a flourishing bow, Nick presented her with the king's letter. Ignoring her mother's morning litany: "Polly, where is your cap?" she took the paper knife Ned offered and carefully slit the magnificent royal seal.

She skimmed the lines, in a neat secretarial hand, expressing fulsome gratitude for her part in saving the Royal Person from a treasonous plot. Then she read the last two lines, above the sprawling signature, "George Rex," and sank into the nearest chair with a gasp.

"It's an invitation to the coronation! For me! To see the king crowned," she babbled incoherently.

"The coronation!" exclaimed her mama. "Good gracious, what an honour. Are you sure you read it right, Polly?"

"You deserve it," Nick assured her. "Jupiter, that'll be something to tell the fellows on the *Steadfast*."

Ned congratulated her, then turned at once to practical matters. "It's lucky the coronation is on the nineteenth. I'm sure you will be able to stay at Stafford House with Nick and me."

"You will need a new gown," Sylvia said. "We shall go shopping tomorrow."

"Don't lose the invitation." Mrs. Howard was determined to find something to worry about. "You had best give it to Ned for safe-keeping."

Polly re-read the letter before handing it to her brother. "I suppose I shall not be able to take my sketch book," she said. "Do you think Kolya has been invited, too?"

Ned read the first few lines. "I imagine so, since he was equally instrumental in saving the king's life."

"Let's go to Mr. Lay's quickly and find out." Polly jumped up. "He said he will be there early."

She was ready to set out as she was, on foot. Her mother and Sylvia persuaded her to wait for the carriage to be brought round, and to don spencer, gloves, and hat. She sat on the edge of the seat all the way to the Steyne, and hopped out of the carriage before Dick had time to let down the step.

Mr. Lay's shop was decked out with a green and white striped awning and a red stuff carpet across the pavement. Polly stood staring at a billboard with her name in large letters (and "under ROYAL PATRONAGE" still larger), until Ned stepped out behind her and took her arm.

"I'm very proud of you, Poll," he murmured.

She looked up at him with shining eyes. "It's really true. I can hardly believe it."

"Let's go in."

"But Mama and Sylvia . . ."

"Nick will bring them. This is your day."

Mr. Lay appeared in the doorway, beaming, with Kolya's tall figure behind him.

"Come in, Miss Howard, come in. I trust my arrangements will meet with your approval."

As Kolya stood aside to let her pass, he whispered, "In your eyes are stars, Polly. Next project must be self-portrait."

All her pictures had been simply framed and hung at eye level, landscapes alternating with portraits and flower studies to lend variety. Here and there were groups of gilt chairs with red plush seats, to encourage the ladies to linger. A small table in one corner bore a vase of yellow roses.

Polly turned to Kolya. "Stolen from the king's gardens?" she enquired in an undertone.

"But of course."

"Did you receive an invitation to the coronation this morning?"

His grin faded. "Yes," he said shortly, frowning.

"So did I." Polly wondered why he was displeased, but today nothing could spoil her elation. "Is it not splendid? Ned says I shall be able to stay at Stafford House with him and Nick. Would it be very improper to take my sketch book to the coronation?"

"Am certain the king will be delighted to see a drawing of his day of splendour. You will allow me to be your escort?"

She drew a deep breath, trying not to burst with happiness. "Oh, yes, please."

Her mother, Lady Sylvia, and Nick joined them at that moment. Mrs. Howard looked around the room and said doubtfully, "Do you think anyone will come?"

"Many of my friends and acquaintances have promised to come, ma'am," Kolya told her.

Mr. Lay, who had been discussing with Ned the pricing of the pictures, also hastened to assure her that any number of his regular customers had begged for invitations to the private opening. "Don't you be worrying, Mrs. Howard, if they come slow at first. 'Tis fashionable to be late." He pulled a huge silver turnip watch from his pocket and consulted it. "Never hurts to open the doors a few minutes early though." He trotted out to the front shop.

The first to arrive were a prosperous merchant and his stout wife. Mr. Lay introduced them to Polly as Alderman and Mrs. Piggott. They looked at her curiously, then went to stare at the two paintings the king had lent.

"You needn't think we'll have the whole city council in here," Mr. Lay assured Polly in a whisper. "No one below alderman, no matter what they was willing to pay. Can't have the raff and scaff mixing with the nobs."

A pair of gentlemen escorted two ladies into the room. They all knew Kolya, and the younger of the ladies at once began to flirt with him. Polly had no time to repine; the older of the gentlemen begged her to be so good as to give him a personal tour of the exhibition. He was exclaiming in admiration over a Brighton panorama, with not a few sidelong glances at the fair artist, when Alderman Piggott's voice was heard.

"If it's good enough for His Majesty, it's good enough for me, cost it never so much. Pick whichever you fancy, Mrs. Piggott, and we'll hang it by the front door."

Polly was called away from the admiring

gentleman to be introduced to some new arrivals. For half an hour people wandered in and out, and then the boy who stood at the outer door, checking invitations, ran into the room.

"Mr. Lay, Mr. Lay," he called shrilly. "He's come!"

The printseller seized Polly's arm and pulled her towards the door. "He's come. You must greet him at the entrance."

"Who?" she asked, bewildered.

Kolya materialized at her other side. "The king. Lady Conyngham said he will, but I did not tell you as I was not certain."

As word spread, the seated ladies rose and an aisle opened from the door to the centre of the room. Mr. Lay and Kolya hurried Polly out, just in time to make her curtsy as His Majesty's majestic form filled the doorway. And fill it he did, though he seemed not quite as vast as he had in his crimson dressing gown. He was soberly dressed for travelling and undoubtedly wore his stays.

Lady Conyngham followed, on the arm of a nondescript gentleman who turned out to be her husband. The king moved into the exhibition room, the wood floor creaking beneath his weight. Abandoning her lord, the Vice Queen joined her monarch, who proceeded to exchange an affable word with those present whom he knew.

Polly watched, feeling slightly dizzy. The king was not looking at her pictures, but even she was worldly enough to know that his visit was enough to ensure her success. Then he stopped before the painting of the Pavilion at sunset.

"Miss Howard?"

She dashed to his side. "Your Majesty? Sir?"

"Daresay this is the one you were working on when you noticed certain goings-on, eh?"

"Yes, sir."

"Makes my little place into quite a fairy palace, don't it, my lady?" he enquired of Lady Conyngham. "I'll take it." With a nod of dismissal and a regal wave to the bowing and curtsying company, he surged out.

From then on, a constant stream of visitors arrived and departed. Though most of them talked more of His Majesty's amazing condescension than of the exhibition, by the time Mr. Lay closed his door, most of the pictures were sold. Polly was exhausted when she retired to bed straight after dinner.

She told herself that the dispirited feeling that hung over her was simply weariness and a natural sense of anticlimax after the excitement of the day. After all, she was the richer by several hundred guineas, and Kolya was going to escort her to the coronation. What more could she want?

All the same, the image that stuck in her mind when she thought of the coronation was not his request to escort her, but his frown.

20

Kolya frowned as he rode towards Loxwood. Though rain dripped from the brim of his hat, it was not the weather that brought the scowl to his usually cheerful features.

A young farmer trotting towards him dug his heels in to urge his cob to a clumsy canter in his hurry to pass the irascible gentleman.

An invitation to the coronation! Kolya thought in disgust. Polly might be flattered and delighted, but he had counted on a more substantial reward. He wanted to support her in comfort, if not in style, and he wanted to marry her now, not in some distant future when he had made his way in his adopted country. He wanted to wake each morning to find her fair head on the pillow beside him, her dark blue eyes opening to greet the new day with an eagerness to match his own.

Shaken by a sudden longing to hold her in his arms, he made up his mind then and there to ask her to wed him after the coronation, come what might. There must be some way to manage it. Had he not told Polly, when he scarcely knew her, that nothing is impossible?

He began to plan. When he reached the lane which led to Loxwood Manor, he turned instead towards the village. Polly, Mrs. Howard, and Nick were staying in Brighton until the exhibition closed at the end of the week, but Ned had gone home to oversee the barley harvest and to give Lord John his notice. He and Lady Sylvia planned to marry at the end of August.

As Kolya hoped, the rain had kept Ned at work in his office instead of out in the fields. He came out to the hall at once, smiling a welcome, on hearing Ella's "Why, if it isn't Mr. Volkov! Come in out of the wet, sir, do."

"Kolya, I didn't expect to see you here. Come into my office. Ella's given me a fire as a treat this miserable day."

"If you aren't soaked to the skin, sir! You'll catch your death. Off with that coat this instant and Mrs. Coates'll have a nice hot cup of tea for you in two shakes of a lamb's tail."

"Thank you, Ella, that will be welcome." Kolya felt as if he were already one of the family. "But do not be concerned for my health. Recall that in Russia we have six feet of snow six months of the year."

"That's as may be. You're an Englishman now, sir," said the maid firmly, and bore off his topcoat to the kitchen.

Following Ned to the office, Kolya said laughing, "Perhaps my preference for England over other nations of Europe is only because, like Russians, you drink tea at all hours." He stood with his back to the fire, his buckskins steaming. "I am on my way to the manor. Ned, you have told John you will leave?"

"Yes. His lordship was kind enough to say he doesn't know how he will go on without me."

"I have big favour to ask."

Ned leaned back in his desk chair and crossed his legs. "Go ahead."

"I want to ask John to give me your post. I know he will do this, for he thinks self in my debt still, but I cannot run Loxwood without your advice. You will be busy with a new family and with Westcombe. Is too much to ask that you help me also?"

"My dear fellow, of course not. I shall not be so far away that I cannot come over for a day now and then. If you were not already familiar with the land and the people I should not think it possible, but it may do very well."

"You can guess why I am in a hurry?"

"Polly? I may have been drunk at the time, but I do remember your saying you wanted to marry her."

"I cannot wait."

"I know how you feel." Ned's grin was sympathetic.

Ella brought in the tea tray, shoving aside her master's papers to set it on a corner of the desk. Kolya sat down and helped himself to one of Mrs. Coates's scones.

"This," his gesture embraced the small whitewashed room and the rest of the small whitewashed house beyond, "this is not the home I have imagined for my bride. You are not offended? I do not mourn the splendour of my father's mansion, you understand — would not suit my Polly — but had hoped for something . . ." He shrugged, unable to find the words.

"Something more in keeping with your station in life. Don't forget that Polly has been perfectly contented living here."

"Is true."

"And my little sister's earnings are growing quite substantial, are they not? At least one of her pictures was marked at a hundred guineas."

"This money will of course be her own," said Kolya decidedly. "To spend for the little comforts and frivolacies which women like. Or to save for our children. Though my son will never be Prince Volkov, I hope we will have children, but this also worries me. Polly must be free to paint, so I will have to hire nursemaids and governesses."

Ned flushed. "I'm sure Sylvia will want to help. She is embarrassingly wealthy, you know, and neither of us plans to cut a dash in society. She is very fond of Polly and admires her painting."

Had they been standing, Kolya could not have resisted embracing his future brother-in-law Russian style, with a hearty kiss on each cheek. "My friend, for Polly I will forget pride and accept help with greatest gratitude," he said emotionally. "Also, my father will perhaps send money now and then. We shall contrive!" He paused, suddenly recalling the one possibility he had not taken into account. "If she will marry me. Ned, do you think she will marry me?"

Frowning, Ned said slowly, "If you had asked me a fortnight since, I should have said yes, yet I cannot forget how she refused to see you the day after your adventure in the Pavilion. She swore you had not made any improper advances . . ."

"I did not!" It was Kolya's turn to flush.

". . . but her nerves were thoroughly overset."

Kolya explained Lady Conyngham's insistence to the king that he and Polly must marry, and Polly's reaction.

"That doesn't sound hopeful," Ned agreed. "Still, she has shown the most unusual sensibility ever since you appeared in our lives. She always had the most equable disposition before. That may be a good sign."

"Or bad." Kolya sagged back in his chair. "What shall I do if she rejects me again?"

"Keep trying," was the only suggestion Ned could offer. Gloomily, Kolya took his leave and rode on through the rain to the manor.

A letter awaited him, from Prince Lieven. The Russian ambassador and his wife invited him to stay at the embassy in London for the coronation. They had a communication for him from his father.

Kolya was glad to accept their invitation, and his spirits rose still further when John expressed himself delighted to offer him Ned's position.

"Howard has everything running smoothly," he said, "and if he has agreed to advise you I'm sure it will work out, don't you think, Beckie?"

His wife smiled and nodded. John had proudly revealed that she was *enceinte,* and she seemed already to have put on a new matronly dignity. Kolya half expected that one or the other would want to hear of his progress in wooing Polly, but either they were too tactful to enquire or they had forgotten his confidence.

Uncertain as he was of the answer, he was relieved not to be asked.

By the day of the coronation, Polly had not seen Kolya for a week. It seemed much longer. Of course she understood that he was unwilling to continue to enjoy the king's hospitality when His Majesty was gone to London. All the same, she wished he had stayed just to see that the last few days of her exhibition were as successful as the first. Every single picture was sold, and it was all thanks to him.

Leaving their mother at Dean House, she and Nick travelled in Lady Sylvia's carriage to Town, meeting Ned in Crawley on the way. Crossing Westminster Bridge, they drove along Whitehall and Pall Mall before turning into Park Lane. A dozen times Polly wanted to stop to sketch the splendid buildings, especially Carlton House. Its dignified

Classical façade was such a contrast to the exotic Pavilion, it was hard to believe both were the creations of the same prince.

When the Howards reached Stafford House they were welcomed by the duke's butler, Mr. Boggs, an impressive personage with a head like a polished egg. "It's a pleasure to see you again, Mr. Howard," he said, beckoning to a footman. "James, take the Howards to Mrs. Davis's room."

Mrs. Davis, the housekeeper, looked harassed. "We've that many guests up for the coronation I don't know which way to turn," she apologized. "Mr. Howard, you won't object to sharing with your brother, I hope?"

She called a maid to show them to their rooms. There seemed to be miles of passages and stairs. Polly wondered whether she would ever find her way back to the front hall.

To her relief, Ned and Nick were in the chamber next door. Her room was small and plain but comfortable, with a window overlooking Hyde Park. Polly was standing at it sketching when another maid brought hot water.

"There'll be two sittings to dinner, miss," she announced, "there being so many people in the house. Mr. Howard said seven o'clock'll suit, and he knows the way to the steward's room." She bobbed a curtsy and dashed off.

The Howards dined with Mrs. Davis, the duke's steward, secretary, and chaplain, the governess of Lord Danville's children (Lady Danville, the wife of his Grace's heir, never travelled without her children), and the duchess's companion, Miss Carter.

"I generally have a tray in my room," Miss Carter confided to Polly, her round face earnest, "when I do not eat with the family, but the servants are run off their feet, poor things, and it seemed unconscionable to give them extra work. Besides, I have a message for you from Aurelia."

"Aurelia?"

"The duchess. She is my cousin, you know. Prince Nikolai dined here yesterday, and they arranged that he shall meet you at the door of the Abbey at nine o'clock, as the Lievens will take him to the coronation. The duke has to go early to be present at His Majesty's robing, so you shall go in the carriage with Aurelia and the Danvilles."

"Thank you, ma'am."

"My dear, do you have a suitable gown?" Miss Carter asked anxiously. "I do not mean to interfere, but perhaps you will allow me to advise you?"

"Lady Sylvia Ellingham helped me choose one in Brighton, ma'am, but I shall be glad of your opinion."

Miss Carter was pleased to approve Polly's pale green sarcenet with white muslin ruffles and the headdress of a garland of white silk roses with green leaves. "The court ladies will wear ostrich feathers, of course, but this is by far more suitable in your position. You will do very well, Miss Howard."

As the little lady bustled out, Polly hung up her gown, then sank onto her bed. "In your position," Miss Carter said. In the excitement of seeing London and looking forward to the coronation, she had not spared a thought for her position. Her family had dined in the steward's room, while Kolya, yesterday, had evidently dined with the ducal family. It was too easy to forget that he was a prince.

How would he feel, the day after tomorrow, escorting a female who as befitted her position was not wearing plumes? Would he be ashamed of associating with her before that glittering company? Was that why he had looked so annoyed when she asked him whether he had been invited to the coronation?

It was no use trying to persuade herself

that he had offered to squire her because he wanted to. He had done it because he was the kindest, most obliging gentleman in the world and knew that she would not "do very well" on her own. He would have done as much for any acquaintance. He must have been hoping that she would refuse. Perhaps she ought to have, yet she was glad that she had not.

The coronation might be the last time she would ever see him. Afterwards she would go to live at Dean House and Westcombe; all connexion with the Danvilles would be over and there would be no reason for Kolya's path to cross hers.

She was going to enjoy the coronation if it killed her, Polly decided fiercely. She was going to revel in resting her hand on his arm, in sitting close to him, in seeing the amusement in his slanting hazel eyes and hearing his richly rolling Russian 'r's. And when she had said good-bye and thank you, she would go home and put him out of her mind and dedicate herself anew to the solitary life of an artist.

If that prospect, once so enticing, had lost its lustre, she did her best not to admit it.

The next day she succeeded in forgetting her woes in the delight of sketching the elegant streets and squares in the neighbourhood. She also went across the road to Hyde Park and drew Stafford House, intending to paint it when she went home as a gift for the duke and duchess in gratitude for their hospitality.

That night, every half hour from midnight on, church bells pealed and guns roared to remind the king's deafened subjects that he was about to be crowned. Not surprisingly, Polly was wide awake when Mrs. Davis, as she had promised, sent a maid to her at half past six to help her dress. The new gown was soft and cool on her skin, whispering about her ankles. With the maid's assistance, she pinned her hair up in a topknot and fastened the silk wreath around it.

"You look a fair treat, miss," the girl said enviously. "Lor, that's really something, that is, going right into the cathedral and seeing him crowned up close, like. D'you reckon you could make some pictures for us after?"

"Yes, of course. I shall take my sketch book with me, if I am allowed."

"There's breakfast in Mrs. Davis's room, miss."

"I'm not hungry, thank you." Polly's nerves were on edge, and the thought of food made her feel slightly ill.

"Mrs. Davis said you'd say that. She says as you've got to eat, acos likely you won't get nothing more till this evening. You wouldn't want to faint from hunger right in the middle of the cathedral, would you, miss?"

So Polly forced herself to swallow a slice of ham and a muffin. She thought that a cup of tea might soothe her, then rejected it for fear of having to answer a call of nature in the middle of the ceremony.

It was only seven thirty when she finished. The entire household was astir like a nest of ants, rushing purposefully to and fro, and Ned and Nick had already gone out to see the sights. Restless and with nothing to do, Polly decided to go across to Hyde Park to make one more sketch of Stafford House while she was waiting for the duchess.

The park was already swarming with celebrators. There was to be a grand fireworks show for the populace in the evening. To take advantage of the crowds, a city of stalls, marquees, puppet shows, and temporary taverns had risen overnight among the trees. Women hawked gingerbread, and a pieman cried his wares. The scene was irresistible.

Polly filled page after page of her sketch book. She could have done a roaring trade, but as she explained to would-be purchasers, she wanted to combine her drawings into a painting later. Time passed unnoticed, until once more guns roared and bells rang and a man standing near her said to his companion, "That'll be nine o'clock?"

" 'Sright," said the other, consulting a battered tin watch. Nine o'clock, Miss Carter had said. Polly lifted her skirts and fled. She raced across Park Lane, dodging vehicles. Outside Stafford House there was no sign of the ducal carriage. Panting, she scurried up the steps and into the front hall.

The elderly porter in his red and green livery drowsed on his stool. No one else was in sight.

"The duchess," Polly moaned. "Is she gone already?"

"Huh? Whassat? Her Grace an' his lordship an' her ladyship left half a hower gone. They was asking fer you — you'd be Miss Howard? — but no one knowed where you was an' they cou'n't wait."

Polly dropped her sketch book as her heart sank to the very tip of her new green kid slippers. "Oh please," she cried, "call me a hackney."

Grumbling under his breath, the old man lumbered down the steps and waved imperiously at a passing hackney. The driver hauled on the reins and his bony nag gladly halted.

"The cathedral," Polly ordered as she jumped in. "Hurry, please hurry."

She tumbled onto the smelly seat as the jarvey whipped up his horse. For a hundred yards the creature rose to a trot before sinking back into a steady plod. Polly clenched her fists, her nails digging into the palms of her hands through her gloves. She would be late, she would be late, and Kolya would be so angry with her. They might not even be allowed in. If she had caused him to miss the coronation, she would never be able to look him in the eye again. If she was lucky, she thought in an agony of remorse, he would have gone in without her.

Gradually it dawned on her, through her despair, that the streets they traversed were growing emptier and emptier. Surely, even if she was hopelessly late, there should be crowds. Then the hackney stopped. Digging in her reticule for her fare, she jumped down, paid the man, and turned — to find herself on the broad flight of steps leading up to St Paul's Cathedral.

Her shoulders sagged. The cathedral, she had told the jarvey. She could hear her own voice ringing in her ears. She could hear the maid, this morning, talking with envy of the cathedral.

Slowly she started up the steps. Kolya was waiting for her at the doors of Westminster Abbey. She would never see him again.

21

Waiting at the main entrance to Westminster Abbey, Kolya saw Tom Danville's tall form moving towards him through the throng. Behind the equally tall guardsman who was clearing a path, the Duchess of Stafford, her daughter-in-law, and Polly were still invisible. As they came closer, he saw the duchess, her ostrich feathers nearly as tall as she was, and then Lady Danville. Shading his eyes, he searched for a glimpse of Polly. He had wonderful news for her.

"Your Grace, my lady." Impatiently he bowed over their hands. "Danville, where is Miss Howard?"

"The silly chit did not turn up when we were ready to leave, Prince," the duchess said crossly. "Neither Boggs nor Davis could find her and we could not wait."

"Sorry, Volkov," said Lord Danville, "but no one had any idea where she had gone." Another group moved up behind them. "We'll have to go in now. Do you go with us?"

Kolya was ready to wager he could guess, if not where Polly was, then what she was doing. No doubt she would turn up, breathless, in a hackney in a few minutes. How he would tease her!

"No, I shall wait here," he said.

Lady Danville laid her hand on his arm. "I do hope she comes in time," she said earnestly.

The three went on into the Abbey. The stream of guests and dignitaries continued to flow past him in swirls and eddies, now and then casting up someone he knew to exchange a few words. The flood began to slacken. One of the guards came up to him.

"We'll have to close the doors soon, sir. Make sure everyone's settled before the procession arrives."

Kolya nodded. She was not coming. His only reason for attending the coronation was to enjoy her pleasure in the colourful pageantry. The king would never notice his absence. He remembered how he had defied protocol in St Petersburg to take Rebecca Ivanovna home early from the tsar's midsummer fête — there was far less cause to dread King George's wrath.

He waited until the great doors swung shut, then pushed his way through the crowd and found a hackney to take him to Stafford House.

It was several minutes before anyone answered the door bell. A footman in the green-and-red livery which reminded him of his Preobrazhensky uniform opened the door and said firmly, "No one's home, sir. They's all gone to the crownation."

"Miss Howard is not here? She did not come to Westminster Abbey."

"I don't know, I'm sure, sir. I'll 'afta ask Mr. Boggs."

Waiting in the grand circular vestibule with its pink marble floor and pillars flanking each doorway, Kolya paced impatiently. Then he caught sight of a familiar object on a side table. Polly's sketch book. He picked it up and flipped through it. Page after page of celebrating Londoners met his eye — he was right, she had been drawing and had forgotten the time. But she must have come back to the house to leave this. Where on earth had she gone?

Mr. Boggs hurried in, buttoning his coat, followed by Mrs. Davis straightening her cap.

"Beg pardon, sir," said the butler, "we was just putting our feet up, as you might say, with everyone gone. You're looking for Miss Howard? I'd know if miss came in, sir."

"She's not here," the housekeeper confirmed. "Will I send for the maid who helped her this morning, sir? Could be she said something."

The maid was sent for. "Miss told me she wanted to draw pitchers of the crownation, sir, if they'd let her," she said. "She promised to show 'em to me. Fine as fi'pence she were in her pretty new frock. For sure she was meaning to go to the cathedral."

Kolya laughed. "Expect she went to cathedral," he said. He could imagine her, rushed and flustered, the word "cathedral" uppermost in her mind after the maid's morning chatter. That was what she would have told the jarvey, and in the unfamiliar city she would not have realised she was going the wrong way.

Enlightenment hit Mr. Boggs. "You mean St Paul's, sir!"

"Is other cathedral in London?"

"No, sir, that's it."

"Then to St Paul's I go." He gave the confused maid a shilling.

The butler himself condescended to summon a hackney, a feat he somehow accomplished simply by raising his chin at it. "I'm sure I hope you find miss safe and sound, sir," he said as he ushered Kolya into the vehicle and closed the door. "A right pleasant-spoken young lady, if I may be so bold."

Any hackney favoured by Mr. Boggs was bound to be above average, and this one set off at a fair clip. Kolya had no idea how far behind Polly he was. Even if he had guessed right, there was no reason to suppose she would still be at St Paul's when he arrived. If only she had taken her sketch book with her, he could have been certain to find her there. Despite her disappointment at missing the coronation, nothing would have stopped her drawing the great cathedral, he thought with a smile.

The hackney slowed as they started up Ludgate Hill. Kolya could not bear sitting still any longer. He paid the driver and strode along the quiet street, all business halted for the celebrations, towards the dome looming over the surrounding buildings.

As he approached Sir Christopher Wren's masterpiece, he paused a moment to admire its splendid simplicity, so different from the ornately Gothic Westminster Abbey. Almost he wished he had brought Polly's painting equipment for her, so that she could sit right down and start on a picture. He grinned — no, this was no time for painting. If she was here, he had other things in mind for her.

Entering the church, he crossed himself in the Russian fashion and looked around the vast, hushed space. No sign of Polly, or anyone but an old man sitting in a pew nearby, who stood up creakily and came towards him.

"Can I help you, sir?"

"I look for a young lady."

The verger frowned in suspicion. "This is no place to be looking for the ladies, young man."

"My sister," Kolya improvised. "She is needed at home. Is fair, with dark blue eyes." He wished he had thought to ask the maid the colour of the new gown.

"Could be her up in the Whispering Gallery," the old man admitted grudgingly. "I'll show you the stairs, but just you remember this is a house of God. There's to be no funny business, mind."

"What is Whispering Gallery?" Kolya asked, intrigued, as he walked beside the verger down the aisle.

The question earned him another suspicious look, but an explanation followed. "A whisper against the wall can be heard right around the other side. Here, you go up here."

And there she was, not twenty yards from

him, sitting on the floor with her back to the wall, her knees clasped in her arms. Even at that distance he could tell that her gaze was fixed on an interior vision — she was planning a picture.

He leaned close to the wall. "Polly," he whispered. She started, looked around in bewilderment, then saw him striding towards her. Her eyes filled and a forlorn tear trickled down her cheek.

He had never seen her cry. He broke into a run and a moment later was seated beside her, pulling her into his arms. "Polly, *lyubimaya moya,* do not weep."

"I'm so sorry," she gasped. "I made you miss the coronation. I don't know how I could have been so stupid."

"I do not care for coronation." He held her a little away so that she could see his teasing smile. "Was not stupidity, *dushenka.* I know just how happened." He told her his deductions.

"Yes, it was just like that. But how could you guess?"

He took out a handkerchief and dried her eyes before pulling her close again. "Was easy. I know my Polly. You will marry me, *dushenka?*"

She stiffened. "I don't want to be a wife, I want to be a painter," she said in a small un-

326

certain voice, but she did not try to escape his embrace.

"Is possible to be both," he said, with a soft laugh. "I promise I will never let anything interfere with your work, *golubushka*. Except that I hope you will not insist on painting in bed."

Though she blushed, she looked up with a twinkle in her eyes and said, "I only sketch in bed," then buried her red cheeks in his shoulder when he laughed again. "What does *golubushka* mean, Kolya?"

"My little dove," he said tenderly. "*Dushenka,* my soul. *Lyubimaya,* my beloved. But this is not time for Russian lesson. You will marry me?"

"Oh yes. And I will try to be a good wife and . . . and mother, but you must not mind if I am sometimes absentminded. Besides," she added, sitting up straighter, "we shall need the money I earn. Perhaps I should paint more portraits. I prefer landscapes but portraits pay better."

"You will paint just what you want, my practical Polly. I have news. My father has sold an estate of three thousand serfs and sent me the money. Already I have made offer on estate next to Westcombe. You will like to live there?"

"Oh Kolya!" She threw her arms around

his neck. "Is it true? Right next to Ned and Sylvia? I cannot imagine anything better."

"I show you something better." Even if they were in a church, he could no longer resist kissing her. Her lips were sweet, her body soft and yielding in his arms, and the way she clung to him promised a passion equal to his own.

"Ahem!"

The verger stood at the top of the steps, glowering at them. With one accord they jumped to their feet. Kolya smoothed his hair and Polly her skirts and they moved forward to lean on the balustrade. The verger stumped around the far side of the gallery, casting black looks at them as he went.

The sun's rays poured into the building until the great dome above them seemed to float in a sea of light. A familiar, faraway look entered Polly's eyes.

"Do you think they would let me paint in here?"

"I will arrange," Kolya promised recklessly. "All is possible."

"Thank you, dearest." Tearing her gaze away from the architectural glories and transferring it to the long, lean, lithe length of him at her side, she touched his cheek. "I have always considered it most unfair," she mused, "that male artists are allowed, indeed expected, to draw female nudes from life. I don't suppose . . ."

"This too I will arrange," he said grinning and, to the verger's horrified disgust, he caught her to him and kissed her again.